ADVENTURES and MISADVENTURES OF DR. SONJEE

A Collection of Short Stories

Prasanna K. Pati, MD

Snehalata Press   Salem, Oregon

Snehalata Press
Salem, Oregon

Printed in the United States of America

First Edition

ISBN: 0-9703820-1-4

Library of Congress Card Number: 00-111880

Design and production by DIMI PRESS

DEDICATION

I had embarked on the P & O. Corfu leaving Mumbai (Bombay) on June 20, 1952 on my way to America. The monsoon was just breaking, and the Arabian Sea was wild. Little did I know that my father lay on his deathbed just five days after I had said good-bye to him on June 18, 1952. I have never been able to resolve that emotional trauma. There has been no closure neither will there be any.

I dedicate this book to my late father, Mr. Mrutyunjoy Pati of Sambalpur, India.

PREFACE

After a long career as a psychiatrist, I started writing short stories as a sort of self-entertainment. I am originally from the State of Orissa in India. Many Indo-Americans from Orissa have urged me to get these stories published as a collection. Also, some of my American friends have enjoyed these stories. Many of my stories deal with conflicts, tragedies, pain, racial issues, Hindu mysticism and beliefs.

In all my stories, Dr. Sonjee is either the story teller or a major character. He is originally from India, but a practicing psychiatrist in America. I played the role of Dr. Sonjee in the classic movie, 'One Flew Over the Cuckoo's Nest' in 1975. Other than that, all my stories are just that: stories

Prasanna K. Pati, MD

FOREWORD

Dr.Sonjee, a psychiatrist from India now living in the United States, is the main character of this book of short stories. Although he is featured on every page, Dr. Sonjee is not the central focus of the book. The humanity of mankind overshadows any individual person and drives the plot. This theme unfolds to become the heart of each story through circumstance, encounter, and dialogue.

In each story, Dr. Sonjee has a private practice in a different city in North America. Whether it is Philadelphia, San Francisco, Toronto, New Orleans, or Montreal, he never remains long in any one place and travels frequently between North America and India for psychiatric meetings or visits wth family or friends. Despit the fact that Dr. Sonjee is forever moving about, staying in hotels or traveling on airplanes, transience and impermanence are balanced with an aura of what remains ageless: the spiritual mysteries of ancient India and the enduring value of friendship.

Each story takes us to a different location. Movement from one city to another in North America, or between India and the United States, is offset with movement between memory and dream, imagination and reality. From the supernatural to the natural world, the reader dwells within the powers of remembrance and friendship. The enduring values of love and brotherhood unfold, surpassing boundaries of race or culture.

Like Albert Schweitzer who left Europe for Africa to heal the hearts and souls of anyone who asked for his help, Dr. Sonjee gives hours of his time listening to any stranger he might meet during his travels. Talking with an old man who is about to die, a young woman whose family perished in Auschwitz, a middle-aged man who has recently lost his wife, a woman who lived as a Sati in a former life, or an elderly Pakistani saddened because he cannot return to the grave sites of his ancestors, Dr.Sonjee opens his heart and gives his time, nothing more. Ironically, healing takes place not because Dr. Sonjee is a psychiatrist, but because he offers the simplicities of human warmth and compassion to others. It is these qualities, not professionalism, that allow catharsis, healing, and transformation to unfold. Each one of us could change the world if only we would slow down, open up our hearts, and truly listen to others.

"Sonjee" was the name given to Dr. Pati in the movie, "One Flew Over the Cuckoo's Nest" in which the author played the part of a psychiatrist.

Linda Hathaway Bunza, Director
Columbia Research Institute for
the Arts and Humanities and
former Editor, *Harvard Education Review*

CONTENTS

THE WOMAN FROM GEORGIA

1609 Peach Avenue,
Atlanta, Georgia 30332

Dear Doctor Sonjee:

Namaskar. It was my pleasure and good fortune that I met you on the Delta flight from Chicago to Atlanta. It seemed almost ordained by God that I would meet a person from Orissa, and a devotee of Lord Jagannath. Aren't you ashamed that you gave me a loving kiss when we parted company in the airport? I have to admit that I liked it, being kissed publicly by an Oriya Brahmin.

Never mind that I am a white female from Georgia, who has never been to India.

You remember all the details that I narrated to you on the flight.

You remember your promise to me. I will wait for you. Love and best wishes.

Sincerely,

Marilyn Benson

It was a summer afternoon in 1985. 1 was busy seeing my patients in my Columbus, Ohio office. It was a long, long day. It was about three in the afternoon when the mailman came. I would always interrupt my routine to check the mail, specifically for letters from India. Even if I have been away from India for so many years, I missed the sights, sounds and my people in India. Thus, a letter from India was always welcome.

The above letter from Atlanta was certainly a surprise. For the moment, it was a blur in my memory. It had been almost two months since I was on that flight to Atlanta. I tried to recall the woman and the conversation. Slowly, I could visualize her charm, and the southern drawl, intensity in her expressions and above all, bits and pieces of her story. I began to laugh at the utter craziness of this encounter, her captivating charm over me and my implanting a tender kiss on her cheek when we parted company. Then, I began to get agitated as I recalled her story. For the moment, I put away from my mind what she told me on that flight and went on seeing my patients.

The last patient left my office around 7 that evening. It was a very hot day in Columbus. I left my office and went on a long walk near the Ohio State University campus, which was not far away. I tried to piece together all the conversation on that flight and finally, my promise to her, which she alluded to in her letter. Being a psychiatrist, I have heard many strange stories, but this one from Marilyn was beyond my wildest imagination and yet, I couldn't shake it off.

We sat together on that flight. I recalled I was reading a magazine from India. I didn't pay any attention to my right, though I was aware that she was very attractive. I recalled she was reading the Chicago Tribune. After several minutes, she had asked me, "Are you from India?" I had just said "Yes" and remained silent. She persisted, "What part of India?" I simply added "Orissa". Only at this point, I made eye contact with her, and again, I was struck with her beauty and I felt uncomfortable, and started looking at the magazine again. I was hoping she would leave me alone, but then the question "What part of Orissa?" I relaxed, as I thought I was with someone who knew Orissa. I asked her, "Have you been to Orissa?" There was a long pause. She was looking out at the sky through the window and I persisted, "What part of Orissa have you been to?"

I will let the reader listen to her story as she told me on that flight .

"No, I have never been in Orissa. I would rather not go to Orissa. You see, I have been there in one of my previous lives. Do not laugh at me. I mean it. You think I am crazy, don't you? You know Dr. Sonjee you are an Oriya. You recall that the custom of Sati Daha, the widow burning in Orissa was not banned until 1829 by the British Government. It was the summer of 1812 that my husband died in the village of Veer Ramchandrapur."

I interrupted her, "You mean, in your previous life and in that village, you became a widow." She simply said with an intensity and sincerity in her voice, "Yes, I became a widow at the age of 19. It is a very beautiful village, mostly a Brahmin village. As per the custom, I became a Sati, that is, I placed myself on the pyre before it was ignited." I remember getting very agitated and almost angry. I told her, "I do not want to listen to such a bizarre and made-up story." She quickly held my right hand and gave it an affectionate squeeze and simply said "Can I go on?"

"I sat on the funeral pyre praying to Lord Jagannath. All the rituals had to be gone through. I was dressed in a colorful red silk sari. I looked at the face of my departed husband. I had been married only four years. I looked at the mango grove by the pond. I saw a number of priests. I knew that some had come down from Puri. I could hear full throated voices shouting "Jai Jai, Jagannath". At a distance, I saw a British officer talking with some priests. I knew that the British authorities in Orissa disapproved of the custom of Sati, but couldn't prevent it by law. Finally, after all the rituals, the time came. You know, according to your customs, the eldest son is to light the funeral pyre, but my son Arjuna, was only a year old. Thus, the duty fell to my brother-in-law. At a distance, I scanned the crowd and saw my son held by my mother-in-law. Only, at that moment, I felt that intense pain that I was leaving an orphan only a year old. For a moment, I felt like bolting from the pyre to hold my son, but amidst deafening cries of "Jai Jagannath", my brother-in-law was coming step by step accompanied by priests and then, he lit the pyre. I also shouted 'Jai Jagannath' and then, I could see and feel the flames around me."

I held her hands, and looked at her face. She was calm and with just a hint of tears. "I have gone through births and re-births since then. But, I cannot forget my son, that little toddler that I left in Veer Ramchandrapur. That scene intrudes my consciousness almost daily. The pain that I suffered from leaving my son is still there." I faintly said, "You know it is difficult to believe your story, but just listening to it, I also feel the pain." She went on, " I can understand your disbelief, I want you to do me a favor." I responded, "If I can." She said, "No, promise me that you will do it." In an unguarded moment and being overwhelmed with her story, I said "Yes." She continued ," I want you to go to that village, Veer Ramchandrapur. It is not very far from Pipli. I want you to talk with the elders there and find out what happened to my son, Arjuna. If you do not believe my story, you go to the office of the District Magistrate in Puri and look at the records of 1812. All I know that the British Government used to keep meticulous records. You may find a description of that event. Yes, I forgot to tell you. My name was Soudamini and my husband's Ratnakara. Yes, find out about my boy and come see me."

The captain was announcing that we were approaching Atlanta International Airport. In a few minutes, we would land. I was speechless. I couldn't think. Here was this strange woman giving me a job to do and then, report to her. The plane landed soon after. We walked together to the baggage claim area, each engrossed with thoughts.

When it was time to say "Good-bye", I gave her a kiss and she gave that affectionate squeeze of my hand and said "You have promised and I will be waiting for you."I took out my business card and gave it to her.

It was not until 1987 that I went to India on a brief visit. But I had never gotten over that story on the flight. I had kept that letter from Atlanta, Georgia. Prior to my trip to India I had thought that I should really tear up that letter, but I just couldn't. Something in me prevented me from doing so. I decided that I might as well visit Veer Ramchandrapur for a day. It is not too far from Puri and in my trips to India, I always go to Puri and the great temple of Jagannath.

It was exactly December 10, 1987 that I took a taxi to that village. I had related the purpose of my visit to some of my family members and they all thought I had gone crazy to pursue a story like that. Finally, one of my distant cousins, who was a devotee of Jagannath, was willing to accompany me, for he too thought there might be something in the story. He was one of those who believed in the super-natural and the unreal.

It was a cool day. I was really struck with the lay-out of that ancient village, a broad street with neat little houses on both sides. We walked in the main street just enjoying the scene. Each house had a garden area and backyard with coconut, mango and guava trees. At the end of the road, there was a temple for Lord Shiva, the Hindu God of Destruction. My cousin suggested that we might meet some village elders in the temple court-yard that we could talk to.

We went to the temple court-yard and then, to the inner sanctum to offer our prayers to Lord Shiva and then, came out. In one corner of the court-yard, there were four elderly men playing cards. We came near them, sat down. There were no enquiries, no questions even if we were total strangers in the village. They seemed to be lost in their game. After what seemed to be a long time, my cousin interrupted their game and said, "Sir, please forgive us for interrupting your game. My cousin here has come from America with a story about your village and he would like to know what you know about it." They stopped their game and waited.

I folded my hands in reverence and told the elders the entire story. I could notice the anxiety in their faces, but there were no interruptions. I finished the story and asked them, if during their childhood, they had heard any accounts of Sati from their grand-parents. There was no response. My cousin asked them directly and finally, one of them said the custom was outlawed so long back that none would remember any stories of Sati. I simply stated that I was interested only in that particular Sati episode of 1812, of Soudamini and Ratnakara and their son Arjuna. Finally, one of them suggested that we go and talk with a certain elderly female, who according to them, was close to ninety and the village historian. We asked for direction to that house and left.

By the time we were walking in that street, the word had obviously spread that I had come from America to verify the details of a Sati in 1812 and we were looking for descendants of one Arjuna. We were now surrounded by the village folks, both men and women. Finally, someone shouted "Jai

Jagannath" and there was the cry in unison to Jagannath.

Obviously, the elderly woman had been alerted about our coming and our story. She was waiting in the door for us, greeted us warmly and had us seated. She had her grand-daughter bring us tea and biscuits. We were surrounded by people. I briefly presented to her the purpose of my visit and she said she understood. I asked her, as the village historian, what she knew about the Sati episode of 1812. She paced back and forth and then, she sat down in front of us and narrated the following story to us: "I must have been nine or ten. I used to go to all the village elders and listen to stories about our village. Those stories have come down for generations. There are no written records. You may want to go to Puri to search the records of the English Government for that year. This is what I know. Every year in this village, we used to have a dozen or so Satis until of course, it was banned by the British Government. Some rich folks preferred to take the body and the widow to the Swargadwara in Puri. I am sure, you have been there, the holy cremation site on the beach at Puri. Here in this village, we have our cremation site near that mango grove by the pond. I was told that the Sati took place there. I was also told that some widows would jump out of the fire, start screaming but be pushed back to the funeral pyre. Mostly, they went along, as that was the custom and ritual of our faith."

I interrupted her and asked her if she had heard anything about my story. She remained silent for a few minutes and then said, "Ratnakara and

Soudamini are common names in our village, so also, Arjuna. You know, it has been almost two hundred years. I do not remember being told about this particular Sati in 1812."

Several persons in the audience came forward to offer stories they had heard about one Arjuna, the infant son of a Sati, but the old woman just declined any comments.

Obviously, it was disappointing that I couldn't find anything about Arjuna. What could I tell Marilyn? Then I and my cousin took a walk toward the cremation site in Veer Ramchandrapur. It was about half a mile. I imagined that Soudamini must have trodden the same path when her husband's body was being taken to the cremation site. It was the same path that many Satis in this village had gone but never came back. Sure enough, there was the mango grove and the pond. I reassured myself that at least I could tell Marilyn about the village, the cremation site, mango grove and the pond, just the way she had described. Finally, we arrived at the exact area where the cremations would have taken place. I stood there, trying to project myself to that day in 1812. It was real as well as unreal. For a moment, I became dizzy and sat down. I touched the soil and then, I cried out to the heavens: "Marilyn".

It was the next day that my cousin and I turned up at the District Magistrate's office in Puri. It took us almost three days to get permission from the authorities to search for the records that I was looking for. And it took another couple of days to locate the bound volumes of the ancient records kept meticulously by the then British authorities. Finally, my cousin and I found the 1812 records. It was amost insane going through those faded ancient English records. I wondered what and why I was doing all this. However, my cousin was always encouraging and optimistic. And lo and behold, there was a volume entitled "Sati in Puri District, 1812." I started trembling, couldn't bear to look at it. I felt like fainting. My cousin took over at this point. After an hour we came across the entry under the village "Veer Ramchandrapur." He slowly read it to me. The entry was dated June 9, 1812. It read, "I had a report from village Veer Ramchandrapur that there was going to be a Sati in the afternoon and that one, Ratnakara had died and that his widow would die in the funeral pyre. I immediately asked for a dozen constables to accompany me to the village, which was about 25 miles from Puri. I hoped to dissuade the priests from this murder, though I had no legal authority to stop it. With haste, we proceeded to the village and luckily, I was there on time at the cremation site with the police force. The widow had just come along with her husband's dead body.

She was stunningly beautiful in a red silk sari. She was so young, almost like a teenager. All arrangements were being made by the priests for the ritual of Sati. I immediately went up to the chief priest and engaged him in a conversation and appealed to him to stop the proceedings. The crowd surrounded us. I could feel the hostility and the agitation in the people around us. My small police force, under my instructions, stayed away in the distance. I appealed to the crowd to save the woman. I appealed to them not to condone a murder. I even threatened them with jail. The crowd was getting restless. I couldn't quite understand the Oriya being spoken around me, but I knew there was anger and hostility. Finally, a spokesman emerged from the crowd. This chap happened to be an attorney in Puri and I knew him. He calmed the crowd and came near me, shook my hand and said, "Sahib, this is our ancient custom. With this act of supreme sacrifice on the funeral pyre of her husband, Soudamini will go to heaven. Mr. Jenkins, you know that your Government does not interfere with our customs. There is no law to prohibit this sacred act. Our people will not tolerate your interference and if you do, there will be bloodshed. The Governor-General in Calcutta and his Council will not approve of your interference". His voice was like steel. He knew what he was talking about. He knew I didn't have the legal authority to stop it. I withdrew with my force and watched the whole scene with complete helplessness. I knew the couple had left a baby boy. In the distance, I saw a woman holding a baby in her arms. I asked my assistant to go and verify if the baby boy belonged to Ratnakara and Soudamini. He came back confirming that it was so. It was almost evening when I returned to my quarters in Puri. I had a sleepless night. I wondered what kind of country this was and why we were here. I prayed to God asking for forgiveness that I couldn't stop an act of murder."

Signed/William Jenkins

My cousin went through a few more pages and then, came across the following entry dated July 27, 1812: "I came to Veer Ramchandrapur on an official visit. There have been reports of dacoits roaming around at night and frightening the people of Veer Ramchandrapur and the surrounding villages. After discussing the matter with the village elders, I directed actions to be taken and ordered the local constables to recruit extra help from the villages to police during nights. After settling this matter, I asked the elders to take me to the house of Ratnakara and Soudamini. I wanted to see the little boy. Ratnakara's elderly father greeted me in the door, had me seated. I asked him if I could see the boy. There was a deafening silence in the room. Then, the old man, through an interpreter, gave me the news that the boy had succumbed to a strange illness a few days after his parents' demise. I was in a state of shock. On my way back, I again wondered what a young devout Christian from Manchester was doing in a country like Hindoostan."

Signed / William Jenkins

We departed with a heavy heart. The beautiful face of Marilyn, that woman from Georgia, danced before my eyes, almost mocking and laughing. Within a few days I was back in Columbus, Ohio and engrossed in my routine. However, I became depressed and started having nightmares all involving scenes of Veer Ramchandrapur. I knew I had to confront myself and go see Marilyn in Atlanta.

It was a beautiful summer afternoon when I knocked at the door of 1609 Peach Avenue in Atlanta. I was met by a young man, who introduced himself as George and said, "Dr. Sonjee, I was expecting you. Come in and please have a seat." I sat down and asked where Marilyn was. "Dr. Sonjee, I am Marilyn's nephew. She passed away about two months back. She had talked to me about you. She thought you might be in India on a project. She passed away rather suddenly. She had told me that you would come to see her. She was expecting some news from you. I guess, you are late." I sat frozen in the chair, then, I got up, agitated. I looked out of the window. I was not sure if the view outside was Atlanta or Veer Ramchandrapur. George came over and hugged me, and added, "Marilyn left a note for you. I will get it." Through misty eyes, I read the note:

"Dear Doctor Sonjee: I know you will be back to see me. I have left instructions to my family that I will be cremated, Hindu style such as the one in Veer Ramchandrapur. Ash is to be collected from the cremation site, placed in an urn. I entrust you with the ash to be carried to Prayag, and disposed of in the Holy Ganges according to your ancient Hindu rites. Do not fail me. I am sure you will bring some news of my son whom I left in 1812. However, I give you the above instructions in case my soul departs to be reborn into another life. Love, Marilyn Benson."

THE CHARRED BODY

I had located my psychiatry practice in the beautiful city of Montreal, Canada in the early 1970's. It is one of the last great cities of North America, where one can still feel the presence of history of days gone-by—a feel of the 17th and 18th centuries. Old Montreal is the oldest Church district in America and even though I am Hindu, I loved to wander around this lovely area.

It was in 1988 that Montreal hosted the International Congress of Jurists. There was a large delegation from India. I had known that one of the members of the Indian delegation was my friend, Justice Tripathy. Of course, it had been more than thirty years since he was my classmate in the Ravenshaw College of Cuttack in the Indian State of Orissa. Justice Tripathy was an eminent member of the Orissa High Court known for his keen legal mind, compassion and honesty but also for his big ego. Though I had not been in touch with him, I was looking forward to a visit with him. He was the judge appointed to inquire into the Hindu-Muslim riots that rocked the city of Cuttack in 1968. I was particularly interested in his findings, opinions and recommendations to the Government of Orissa. I also thought it would be a real opportunity for my friend, Miss Helene Drummond, to learn first hand about the Hindu-Muslim conflicts in South Asia. She was a Professor of Political Science in McGill University of Montreal and a specialist in inter-religious conflicts, be it India, Sri Lanka, Northern Ireland or the Middle East.

I called the organizers of the Congress and left a message for my friend. I was not sure he would find time to visit with us. After all, I had procured a program of the conference, and Justice Tripathy was a panelist in several symposia.

One evening, I received a call from him, "Dr. Sonjee, I received your message. Yes, it will be a great pleasure to visit with you. I am free tomorrow noon. I had known you were in Montreal and I was hoping that we could get together."

We decided to meet at the Maharaja India Restaurant on the Boulevard Saint-Laurent. I had told him that I would bring along a special friend, an expert on inter-religious conflicts around the world.

Helene and I met him in the hotel lobby around noon the next day. "Justice Tripathy, I am Dr. Sonjee. You look good. I would like you to meet my friend, Dr. Helene Drummond, a Professor of Political Science at McGill University, here in Montreal."

For a moment, Justice Tripathy seemed to be a bit confused as Helene, of French-Canadian origin and long dark hair, was in her forties and stunningly beautiful. He regained his composure and said,

"What a surprise, Dr. Drummond. I am delighted to meet you."

I added, "Helene has a Ph.D. from Harvard and her thesis was on inter-religious bigotry."

Helene, who is very outgoing, added, "Call me Helene. Justice Tripathy, I am very pleased to meet you."

We went to my car and started towards the restaurant. In my excitement in meeting my college friend, I started talking Oriya, but Helene quickly responded, "Darling, not in your language please."

Helene and the Justice were conversing very amicably on the current situation in India. He was a bit uncomfortable at the beginning, but soon responded to Helene's warmth, charm, openness and friendliness. We very much enjoyed the buffet lunch which had both North and South Indian cuisine.

"Justice Tripathy, you chaired the Enquiry Commission to go into all aspects of the Hindu-Muslim riots at Cuttack. I think it was 1968. Both Helene and I are very interested in hearing from you firsthand."

Justice Tripathy didn't expect such, as I could see that his expression changed. He avoided eye contact. There was a moment of silence and tension.

"Dr. Sonjee, why should you be interested in your native Orissa? You left for America and decided to stay back. If you had really cared for India, you would have come back and served your own people. You are no longer an Indian. Why would you be interested in the Hindu-Muslim riots of 1968?"

I was not expecting such from Justice Tripathy. He pushed my buttons and I became angry, but maintained my civility.

"Obviously, Justice Tripathy, you do not wish to talk about it. Regardless of what you think, I love India, perhaps, from a distance. Furthermore, what difference does it make if I am a doctor here in Canada or India?   After all, our Hindu scriptures proclaim repeatedly, 'The entire Universe is one family'. Furthermore, I would be lying if I did not admit that I like to be here in Montreal rather than Delhi or Calcutta."

Helene was quiet for a change, with a sort of enigmatic smile. Justice Tripathy did not respond.

Helene interjected, "Darling, perhaps Justice Tripathy has some painful memories related to the Enquiry Commission. You should not press him any further."

I responded, "Helene, you are a scholar on interreligious conflicts beginning with the Crusades, the persecution of Jews for centuries, the raging fires of hatred in the Middle East , Hindu-Buddhist alienation in Sri Lanka, Catholic-Protestant warfare in Northern Ireland, ethnic cleansing of Hindus by terrorists in Kashmir, and frequent Hindu-Muslim riots in India.   Here is an opportunity for us to learn from this eminent jurist. My memory of Cuttack is that it was peaceful. I had Muslim and Christian friends."

Justice Tripathy, at this point, called for the waitress and ordered wine for himself and us.

"Dr. Drummond and Dr. Sonjee, the Enquiry Commission I chaired after the riots is even now most unpleasant to think about. Even now, after so many years, at times I have nightmares. I did not expect a non-resident Indian would be interested in it after some twenty years. After all, India is full of tragedies. Yes, I will tell you about it, not the legal aspects but what I went though as a judge, sifting evidence through truth, lies, distortions, confusion, contradictions and accusations from literally hundreds of witnesses. The city was paralyzed for five days. It was taken over by mad people—riots, stabbings, burning of houses and shops. Do you understand, and can you visualize those scenes?"

The waitress came over with three glasses of wine. He proposed a toast to our health and we reciprocated. He took a sip and proceeded, "Dr. Drummond, are you sure you want to hear all this horrible story?"

Helene responded, "I am a scholar, yes, it will be the first time that I will hear it directly, from an eminent jurist, a first hand account of the inquiry."

"Dr. Sonjee, perhaps you remember some of the localities of the city of Cuttack such as Chandni Chowk, Buxi Bazar, Chowdhury Bazar, Manglabagh, Chauliaganj, Bangla Sahi, Ranihat, Nuabazar. Not a single one of these historic areas escaped the spreading riots."

"Justice Tripathy, " I asked, 'how did it start?"

"It is a good question. I heard all kinds of causes during my investigative inquiry. Even the police didn't have a clear idea. It started in the stadium where there was a soccer match between the visiting

Russian and the Orissa team. How and when and why it became a communal riot was not clearly established. "

Helene commented, "What was the riot like? Was it simple street demonstrations and some sporadic incidents of arson?"

Justice Tripathy did not respond and asked the waitress to bring three more glasses of wine. He sipped the wine slowly. Then he proceeded, "No, Dr. Drummond, from the testimony received at the Inquiry Commission hearings and from police officers, the city went insane —groups of young Hindus proceeding menacingly towards predominantly Muslim neighborhoods and vice versa, stabbings of members of the opposite community and arson. Within a few hours, the police lost control. People who knew each other as friends suddenly became enemies. It was a repetition of what happened in Lahore at the partition of India. Dr. Drummond, you have studied such conflicts from medieval times. You know very well, there is no reason."

"Justice Tripathy, were there fatalities?" I asked.

"Yes, there were fatal stabbings. The police recovered many bodies mostly belonging to the minority Muslim community after the riots had subsided. They were victims of stabbing or cutting the throat. There were also victims whose eyes had been gouged."

Helene interrupted, "Justice Tripathy, I am feeling sick in my stomach. Let us take a break and I suggest, we walk over to the Notre Dame Church. I realize both of you are Hindus and you need not go in, but I need to pray."

We walked in silence to the Church and we entered the inner sanctuary. Helene knelt down and prayed and we, two Hindus, stood just behind her in prayerful silence. In my mind, I attempted a prayer, but nothing came to me.

We came out of the Church and went to its courtyard. We sat on a bench. Justice Tripathy continued, "During testimony given at the Inquiry Commission hearings, I heard such stories for many months. Gradually, I became insensitive. Dr. Drummond, for a judge, it is very, very difficult to establish truth and facts in India. It was gut-wrenching testimony. It was friends and neighbors who had lived in peace for years and suddenly turning against one another just because of religion. Dr. Sonjee, you are a psychiatrist. Perhaps you have some explanation for such brutality."

I responded, "Justice Tripathy, I may call it a mass psychosis or hysteria but that does not really explain it."

The judge continued, "I will just relate two incidents. A man testified that he saw a man stab to death an elderly male of the other community. The assailant suddenly realized that he had called the dying man, 'Uncle' for many years, even though the latter was a member of the other community. According to the testimony, the miscreant, in the dim light, held up the bleeding elderly male, hugged him and reportedly said, 'Uncle, forgive me for what I have just done' as he cradled the dying man to his chest."

Helene interrupted, "According to the testimony of this witness, was there any response from the dying man?"

"Helene, I asked him the same question and the response was a look difficult to describe."

I said, "Justice Tripathy, is this one of the episodes that brings on nightmares to you?"

"Precisely so, Dr. Sonjee. I grew up in a small village near Cuttack. We had a Muslim neighbor, who was a teacher in our school. I used to call him 'Uncle' and his wife 'Aunty'. In our large village we, the Hindus, participated in the Muslim community's Muharram and they, in our Dusserah festivals."

Helene said, "Justice Tripathy, I am shocked. I cannot believe that such cruelty could happen in the land of Gandhi and Buddha."

"It is getting late. Let me come to something that haunts me even after twenty years. During the inquiry, a police officer brought a pair of shoes. It was the kind of shoes worn by Muslim women. He testified that this pair of shoes was found near a female body charred beyond recognition. The body was not claimed by anyone. Several witnesses had testified as to who it might be, but the fact is that it was so charred that it could not be identified. The question was, was she a Hindu or a Muslim woman?"

I interjected, "How did the police dispose of the body? Was there a Hindu cremation or was it consigned to a grave, as per the Muslim custom?"

Justice Tripathy paused for a while. Then, he added, "As the body was burnt beyond recognition and as it couldn't be proven that the shoes belonged to the woman, leaders of both communities agreed to perform both Hindu and Muslim funeral services and thus, she died as a citizen of India, neither Hindu nor Muslim."

It was close to evening. We walked in silence to the flower-decorated square named for the early French explorer Jacques Cartier to listen to outdoor fiddlers playing French-Canadian folk tunes. Our mood soon improved and Helene asked me to join several people dancing to this soulful music.

We took Justice Tripathy to his hotel and Helene, while wishing the Justice good-bye, planted a kiss on his cheek. He didn't expect such warmth and affection, but soon regained his composure and asked Helene, "If I may ask you, are you in love with my friend, Dr. Sonjee?"

Helene didn't expect such a personal question and seemed surprised. I interjected, "Helene, in the culture of India, such personal questions are not considered inappropriate."

At this, Helene started laughing, came close to me, planted kisses on both cheeks, and said, "Dr. Sonjee and I are diverse he, a Hindu from India and I, a French-Canadian Catholic. Justice Tripathy, shall we say, it is Platonic love."

CONFRONTATION

D r. Sonjee had just returned from a visit to India. He had left India many years back, and was now settled in Sugarcreek, Kentucky, on highway 65 not too far from Abraham Lincoln's birthplace. Dr. Sonjee lately has been pensive, moody and at times, depressed. He was considered a competent and respected psychiatrist, having successfully treated many patients but he knew in his heart of hearts that he too occasionally suffered from bouts of depression and alienation, and from the effects of the strange and unexpected twists in life. He wondered how and why a person from a small town in India could end up as a psychiatrist in a relatively unknown but colorful small town in this heartland of America.

But today was different. He felt bouncy and optimistic. He had just returned from an India which was vibrating with changes. The great Prime Minister Gandhi had won the election by a land-slide. Her party's slogan, 'Eliminate Poverty' had caught fire with the electorate. She had also liberated Bangladesh. He recalled, during his visit, how the great Prime Minister was compared to the Hindu Goddess Durga. His friend in India had told him, "Our Prime Minister is a re-incarnation of our Goddess. She has come down from Heaven to clean India of all the evils. Yes, my friend, you people in America will not understand our faith. You just watch her. I think she will cleanse the whole world of evil."

Dr. Sonjee had felt a sense of elation during his visit. Perhaps India was waking up, was finally discarding the shackles of colonialism. He felt so satisfied about his visit. Even if he had abandoned his home country for the greener pastures of America, Dr. Sonjee had always felt proud that he was from India. He smiled to himself, and thought that it was now time for him to educate the American people on the culture and civilization of India, of the great philosophical truths of Hinduism. He got carried away with his plans. He sincerely believed that the American people could profit from the teachings of India. Secretly, he admired America, but being a psychiatrist, he was keenly aware of the vast and complex social problems in America. He decided that he was going to do something about it, by giving talks to various groups who cared to invite him.

It had been almost a year since he had started the project. He had developed a reputation of being a true expert of India's cultural values. He had been invited to various groups and he thought his messages had been appreciated by these groups of American people. His reputation spread beyond the town and to the neighboring states. He had even received an invitation from a small college within

Los Angeles. Dr. Sonjee was pleased with himself that his project was such a great success.

He studied the philosophy of Hinduism. He read the Hindu 'Song of the Lord' daily. In Sugarcreek, he became known as the "Guru, the Teacher". His friends remarked that there was a radiance about him, a sense of joy. Dr. Sonjee now could write to his brothers about his mission, of introducing spiritual concepts to the daily living of Americans. He marvelled at how much he had learned from his patients over the years. He could visualize the faces of many of his patients, and knew he could have helped them more if he had utilized such spiritual concepts.

On his daily walks in Lincoln Park Dr. Sonjee would go over his thoughts very carefully, organizing them into his next speech. Sometimes he also recalled how as a child he was always unfavorably compared with his brilliant elder brothers. His teacher, known as Jack the Fox would ridicule him, and shout at him, "Look at your brother. He is the Golden Boy, and what are you?" He also remembered with some irritation and anger, the sarcastic and taunting remarks of a distant cousin of his father,"Your grades are not good enough. Your school record is not good enough for this family. Why are you wasting your time, reading novels and stories rather than studying?" He could now laugh under the trees of Lincoln Park as he thought about the way he had hidden novels under his textbooks at home, and read them, when no one was watching. He also remembered his total collapse at the college debating society. He had thought he would follow in the footsteps of his elder brother, who was a brilliant speaker. He remembered, with much embarrassment, even now, how he had stood dumb in that debating competition, unable to proceed. Those days were now over. With much satisfaction, he could now claim to be a good speaker.

It was a lazy Saturday. Dr. SonJee as usual was going thru his daily mail. He opened an envelope, reading the invitation carefully. It was a letter from a small town in Texas. A Kiwanis Club of Sweethome had invited him to speak. He had never been to that part of Texas. So he quickly checked his diary, to see if there would be a conflict on the proposed date. He was going to accept the invitation.

Dr. Sonjee was very impressed with Sweethome. He took an early morning walk enjoying the scenes, sounds and activities of the small town America, so different from India. He went over his talk again. He was well prepared, as he was giving the usual speech which was a brief overview of the civilization, history and culture of India. There would also be the highlights from Hinduism. He particularly liked the great humane concepts of Hinduism, 'See Thy Self in Others and others in Self' and also, 'The Entire Universe is one Family'.

Mr. Harris of the Club introduced Dr. Sonjee as an expert of the great culture of India, and a psychiatrist. Dr. Sonjee was full of self-confidence and gave his customary talk with sincerity and feelings. There was applause at the end of his talk, and as he always did, he invited questions. He didn't particularly like this phase of his presentation, the American style question and answer period. He looked around, and there didn't seem to be any stirrings. He was just about ready to thank the audience, and then, he saw a hand go up from someone sitting almost in the last row.

"Yes, you have a question..."

"Dr. Sonjee, my name is John Barber."

"Mr. Barber, go ahead."

"I have a few questions."

Mr. Barber surveyed the audience, looked straight at Dr. Sonjee and asked, "Dr. Sonjee, do you know that there are more Indian psychiatrists in America than there are in India?"

Dr. Sonjee noticed that Mr. Barber was a Black American. He didn't like the question, and he felt uncomfortable.

Mr. Barber didn't wait for the answer, and stated, "Don't you think, after getting your training in America, you should have gone back to help your own people?"

There was a vague murmur going thru the audience. At this point, Mr. Barber stood up and stated, "Doc, you are a shrink, aren't you?"

There were a few chuckles going around. Again, Dr. Sonjee felt anxious, wished it would end. However, he was not about to run even though he didn't like the question. He gathered his courage, looked eyeball to eyeball at Mr. Barber, and asked back, "How are those questions related to my talk?"

Mr. Barber left his chair from the back and came to the front, and looked at the audience, and not at Dr. Sonjee. He turned around and stared at Dr. Sonjee with a smile, "Doc, you know, I am sure, about Hindus and Muslims killing each other in India."

Dr. Sonjee unsuccessfully tried to keep a smile on his face, but he found it difficult to respond. There was no need to as Mr. Barber added, "Yes, more Hindu-Muslim riots, more police shooting at crowds, more killings than British India ever experienced."

Dr. Sonjee felt like screaming or even running away from the place, but being a proud person, he stood there, avoiding the gaze of his questioner.

Mr. Barber came to the podium, and looked straight at Mr. Harris, and added, "'Mr. President, I do not want to embarrass this poor little Indian doctor. He just represents the massive hypocrisy that is India." His voice began to rise, almost shouting at the face of Dr. Sonjee, "Hypocrisy, that is what India is all about; child labor, and what you call, Doc, 'Sati', widow burning or something like that, dowry deaths, your caste system, your considering those low caste folks as sub-human; what caste do you belong to Doc, Brahmin, the priest class I guess."

Dr. Sonjee reluctantly intervened and found himself shouting "India is the largest democracy in the world," but Mr. Barber gave him a cold stare. Dr. Sonjee stopped.

Mr. Barber added, with a low sarcastic, cutting voice, "Yes, Doc, a Brahmin, closer to God than we poor folks, isn't that what you believe?"

Dr. Sonjee had no words of rebuttal. He looked at Mr. Harris pathetically. Mr. Barber then shouted, "Doc, I am a Black. What do you think you are, black or white? You folks from India claim that you are Aryans referring to some migration to India four thousand years back. You don't like to mix with us, the Black folks of America. You hobnob with the white folks. You're too good for folks like us."

Dr. Sonjee refuted in a loud voice, "It is not true, certainly not in my case."

Barber paused, had a sweet smile and then charged, "Doc, from your talk today, I gather you have a flare for history. You know, that your countrymen were driven out of Uganda, Burma and then, Kenya. Do you have an explanation for that? I guess, you don't but I have one: exploitation of the natives, clannishness and isolating themselves socially. Isn't that what the British did in India for two centuries?" Then, he looked at the ceiling as though talking to the Heavens, "Look at my black skin. We black folks have been victimized for three centuries in America. You folks from India are good in business. You also shout from the housetops that the average income of an Indian family in America is more than a white family. Have you ever thought of helping us, Black folks, giving us some opportunities?"

Dr. Sonjee fought back, and shouted at Barber, "Look here, I am not a businessman. I am just a doctor."

Barber wouldn't give up, and shouted back, "You Indians are the Black Jews of America. Do anything for a fast buck."

There was a loud murmur from the audience. Several people stood up and demanded that Barber retract his words. One member came up to Barber, made a threatening gesture, and said "Such prejudicial statements in our club will not be tolerated."

Barber looked at the audience and then at Harris, said with a sincere voice, "I am sorry for what I said. I apologize."

Many members were getting restless and there was an air of agitation.Tension was high but surprisingly, no one had left the room.

Barber finally said, "Doc, my people, the Black people are dying. They are dying of despair. Your Hindu God of Death, Yama, prevails over the inner cities of America. You're a shrink. You understand. You've had a few Black patients in your career. You know how they feel. But most of them can't afford to go to shrinks like you. Just look around. Look with your third eye. You know how to do that."

Dr. Sonjee looked straight at Barber and said, " I treat all patients the same regardless of color, creed, religion or country of origin."

Barber remained tense and agitated for a moment, then he suddenly flashed a smile, came over to Dr. Sonjee to shake hands, and said "Remember Doc, what you said in your talk about a great concept from your Holy Books, 'See Thyself in Others and Others in Self'."

Mr Harris stood up, thanked both Dr. Sonjee and Barber, and terminated the meeting.

It has been many months since he went to Sweethome. He has been regularly declining many invitations to talk, and has become a bit reclusive. He had gone over that meeting many, many times in his mind. Sometimes, while walking in Lincoln Park, he would hear the voice and words of Barber. Barber was always with him. In fact, Barber has become a constant companion to him on his walks, and was frequently engaged in debate with him.

It was a winter evening, cold and with snow on the ground. Dr.Sonjee much enjoyed the varying and beautiful faces of Lincoln Park depending on the season. He loved the solitude of the park, specially in winter. After a full day with his patients, he found that a walk in the park was most relaxing.

He was, as usual, walking and day dreaming, when he was suddenly jolted by a mocking voice from his back, "Nigger, what are you doing over here?" Then, he heard more voices coming from the same direction. He became very apprehensive. Was his mind playing tricks on him? He suddenly heard footsteps behind him, coming closer and closer. Suddenly a pair of hands grabbed him around the chest.

He shouted at them, " I am Dr. Sonjee, a doctor in Sugarcreek. Please leave me alone." He could clearly see three tall youths, and immediately recognized them as 'Skinheads'. He pleaded with them to let go. He heard the mocking laughter, and words such as, "You Hindu, go back to your own country." "You Gandhi, go back to where you came from." Then there was a heavy blow on his head.

Dr. Sonjee has now been in the hospital for several days, recovering from the brain injury. He is slowly improving. He is now able to recognize his family members. He is beginning to realize that he has suffered a brain injury, and the outlook is not yet predictable. His memory is very poor. Sometimes, he can't understand the nurse. At other times he cries, not knowing what he is crying about.

He is lying on his hospital bed early one morning. It is a brilliant sunny day outside. He knows that he is more rational today. He can even daydream about walking in Lincoln Park. His reverie is interrupted by Mrs. Hill, his nurse.

"Dr. Sonjee, the Police detectives have come many times to get information about the incident and descriptions of your assailants. Do you feel like talking with them today?"

Dr. Sonjee faintly replied, "Please send them in." Officers Kelly and Jordan came in, sat down on chairs close to the bed. Officer Kelly admired Dr. Sonjee. He knew Dr. Sonjee as a very competent and compassionate psychiatrist, who once successfully treated his sister out of a severe depression.

Officer Jordan stated the purpose of the interview, "Dr. Sonjee, we want you to recall all the events prior to the assault. More importantly, we would like you to describe the assailants as clearly as you can. This community is shocked at this event, but so far there have been no arrests."

Dr. Sonjee looks at both these officers for a moment, then shifts his gaze to the window. There is that brilliant sunshine. The world outside looks so peaceful and beautiful.

Officer Jordan asks again, "Doc, please help us. We need all the information we can get, for arrests and prosecutions."

Dr. Sonjee recalled those faces of his assailants, their peculiar outfits, and hairstyle, tall young white males, perhaps in their early twenties. He can clearly remember their tauntings and finally, the blunt blow on his head. From that point on, it is a blank.

After several minutes, he spoke in a calm but faint voice, "Officers, you are Christians, aren't you? Do you believe in forgiveness? I am not a Christian, but our Hinduism teaches, 'See Thyself in Others and others in Self'. With that in my heart, I ask God to forgive them. That is my final statement."

He shook hands with both officers, looked out, and wondered whether he was in India or America, or whether he was a Hindu or Christian. He was aware that he was getting confused and that his mind was getting cloudy. He wanted to utter the same name of God that the great Gandhi had just after he was shot by an assassin but he couldn't recall the name of that God. All he could faintly say is 'Ma, Ma, Ma'.

THE GATEWAY TO HEAVEN

Every sunset during my two-week stay in Puri in the winter of 1981, I would walk towards Swarga Dwara, literally meaning Gateway to Heaven, the cremation site on the beach. Puri is famous for the temple of Lord Jagannath, the holy Hindu shrine, a place of pilgrimage for Hindus for centuries. Having been in the practice of psychiatry in Chicago for many years, I was suffering from burn-out, fatigue, and irritability, I thought it was time for me to return to my native Orissa and nothing could be better than to spend a few days in Puri, walking on the beach, visiting the Great Temple, reflecting on the meaning of life and meditating near the cremation site.

During my early morning walks, the beach would be full of bathers, strollers, vendors, fishermen. The Bay of Bengal was shimmering in gold and silver. However, I enjoyed the evening walks with brilliant sunsets and the sky aglow with bright colors. Soon, it would be dark and I would be left alone by hawkers, but families were still lingering or strolling on the beach, enjoying the snacks, perhaps listening to the music of breaking waves.

I would invariably go towards the Swarga Dwara, the cremation site on the beach. There would be funeral pyres, perhaps, half-a-dozen or more. There would be small groups of people huddled together, squatting close to the funeral pyre of a departed loved one and sometimes, a funeral pyre with no one nearby.

As I recall, it must be about the third or fourth evening that I observed a squatting figure at a certain spot. Again, I saw the same figure in the same posture for three more evenings and I began to wonder about this. On the fourth evening, my curiosity overwhelmed me and with caution, I took a few steps towards this unknown creature. It was dark, but there was some light from a nearby funeral pyre and as I approached, I heard voices emanating from this figure, two different voices as if two persons were in conversation. I came to about ten feet from the figure when the voices stopped abruptly for a moment and then, a male voice, quite clear, asked me simply, "Who are you?"

I was speechless for a minute or so, fearful, my childhood memories of ghost stories intruding into my consciousness, this macabre scene of a cremation site on the beach at Puri, funeral pyres nearby, and a psychiatrist being asked a question by a human figure who has been on the same spot for at least four evenings.

I took a deep breath and told him, "I am Dr. Sonjee, a doctor from Chicago. I am originally from

Orissa." At that point, I couldn't proceed, not only speechless but anxious. I was about to run away, but it gave me some solace that there were still clusters of squatters nearby various funeral pyres. I wanted that figure to say something as the silence was unbearable. I wanted to hear some human voice to assure myself that I was in the real world and not in a nightmare. Finally, I could bear no more and shouted in Oriya, "Kichhi Kahantu", meaning, "say something." Then, I heard this very soft and sweet voice, "Please come and sit by me."

I was still apprehensive but sat down on the sand, five feet away from him. Then, I waited. After what seemed to be a never-ending minute, he told me his story about himself. I will put down here more or less what he told me. "Dr. Sonjee, I didn't expect anyone would be curious about me. I have been here four evenings, meditating. I have seen many dead bodies brought in for cremation during these four evenings, sometimes the mourners just a few yards away from me, but none has come as close as you."

I was feeling reassured by this matter-of-fact version and mustered enough courage to speak up, "Sir, when I came close to you just a few minutes back, I heard two voices, as if two people were in conversation, two distinct voices, both male and that aroused my curiosity. Am I correct or was my mind playing a trick on me?"

"Yes, Dr. Sonjee, you are right, you did hear two voices. I was having a talk with Lord Jagannath." At this, I couldn't help but laugh aloud and stated, "Why have a talk with Jagannath here? Why not go to the great temple and face Him there?"

I was increasingly feeling bold in confronting this man, perhaps insane, claiming to be communicating with Jagannath. It was quite dark by now but there were at least three funeral pyres nearby. I saw no one around.

Then, I heard the same voice, "Let me proceed with what I was going to tell you. Yes, I was having a talk with God. Let me tell you my whole story. Do you have time?"

I replied, "Yes, I have plenty of time."

"You see, my name is Ramakanta Panda. I am from Balasore, a retired school teacher. I am almost 75. I am a life-long bachelor. I have no dependents. I get a small pension from the Government. I have no one in Balasore. I have no close friends anywhere. Yes, I have a brother in Cuttack and a sister in Delhi, but I have not been in touch with them for years. I have had no contact with my nephews or nieces. Even during my teaching career, I led a secluded life. I have always been a voracious reader. On retirement, I moved to Puri, to be near Lord Jagannath. I have a small room in a boarding house near the beach."

"You are living a life of detachment, of no desires, no passions and no ambitions," I said.

"Not quite" he responded. "You see, I am a devotee of Lord Jagannath. I visit the temple. I attend all the festivals and festivities. I walk on the beach daily, reflecting on the meaning of life."

"But why meditate here on the cremation site? Why not in the court-yard of the Great Temple?"

He was silent for a moment as if he was pondering an answer and he added, "This is a cremation site. This is the Gateway to Heaven. Truth is no more transparent anywhere than here. I have been on this site on many lonely evenings. I go into a trance-like state. Then I have a conversation with God, our Lord Jagannath."

It seemed to make sense to me. I remained silent. Not too far away, was the Bay of Bengal, the soothing music of breaking waves, the beach almost deserted, a bit scary to be near the shadowy figure of a man who has been in a conversation with Jagannath. I thought to myself, "Why am I here? What am I looking for? Why did I leave the comfort of my suburban Chicago home to come to this unreal scene?"

My reverie was jolted by this particular conversation between two voices, one voice accusing the other of casting a spell over the Oriyas. As I recall, this was the man's voice, which said, "You, the Lord of the Universe, you Kalia, the Black God, you have mesmerized the people of Orissa to the point that they are no longer able to fight for themselves. They are no longer able to take action to correct their problems. All they do is to pray to you over and over again. This great Orissa when your temple was built has fallen into despair and disgrace. Look around your own abode. Your people are unable to stand on their own feet. The large majority are struggling to survive day after day. Where is your mercy and your guidance?"

Then I heard the other distinct voice from Mr. Panda, in response and presumably the voice of God, "You are an angry man. Your rage is boiling over. You feel deeply for your people. That I appreciate very much. You people have built me this beautiful, magnificent temple. You have for centuries developed these elaborate rituals for my worship. You take me on a parade in the Car Festival. You celebrate the festival with wild enthusiasm but my message to you has been lost over centuries."

The first voice, that of the man, responded, "You have failed to guide your people. Visiting you, praying to you and calling your name to help, has replaced all action to improve life, to help each other, and to turn their life around. This once powerful and beautiful country is now like a vast famished land except for a few. Your people do not even realize that they are facing a calamity, an immense tragedy. Your people are under-nourished, they are physically and mentally weak. All they are doing are prayers to you and thus, mesmerizing themselves into inaction and lethargy."

Jagannath responded, "I am deeply distressed at what you are saying. My message has been universal love, not cowardice or inaction in the presence of evil. You know the message of the Gita."

It struck me that the message in the Gita, the essential and the core, is to fight evil, to do right. However, the response of our great God Jagannath didn't sound convincing even to me. I thought for a moment that Gita was quoted profusely all over India but hardly practiced. My own thinking was interrupted by the response of the man, Mr. Panda. "Oh Jagannath, do not quote. I know all about it. Do not hide behind such intellectualization from the Gita. That response will not help our people. I am having this conversation with you and I haven't been wiser. You have to come down from your pedestal in your great temple and arouse your people to action as you were able to do for several centuries. Your people have become weak, passive, inactive, confused and perfectly content with praying to you and blaming either the British or the Muslims for their occupation of Orissa. Your temple has now become a place to hide from the real world."

I was curious to listen to what the Great Jagannath, the Lord of the Universe, would say to Mr. Panda's sharp comments. I looked around and the beach was now almost deserted. However, there were still some funeral pyres aglow. Then, in the distance, I could hear voices and soon enough, another bier was being brought to the beach for cremation. It was close to ten o'clock in the evening. While I was preoccupied with witnessing another body being brought for cremation, I suddenly remembered Mr. Panda but he had disappeared. At that point, I was not sure if I was sane or insane. I looked around some more and all I could see was the bier being placed on the sand with some crying loudly and a few pyres still burning. There was no sign of Mr. Panda. For a moment, I got confused and despite the funeral pyres around me, I thought I was in Chicago. I came back to my senses and started walking towards my beach hotel.

Early the next morning I walked to the temple of Jagannath, which was just a mile away from the hotel. I was in the inner sanctum, worshipped our Great Jagannath with the usual rituals. On another level, I was still trying to sort out my experiences on the beach the previous evening. During the afternoon, I took a long walk on the great road leading to the temple. On a side lane, I entered a small monastery and I was delighted to find a room full of men and women engaged in devotional singing to Lord Jagannath. I sat down on the floor and listened to this soulful music, sung in unison. It was enchanting.

I was on the beach as usual late in the afternoon, walking and enjoying the scene. The sunset was spectacular. I was away in a remote area of the beach. I was debating whether I should return to the Gateway to Heaven, the cremation site. It was beginning to get a bit dark. Then, almost as if in a compulsion, I started walking towards the cremation site. There were already more than a dozen funeral pyres some with a few people around and some with none nearby. I came to the same spot where Mr. Panda was there the previous evening and sure enough, he was there, a shadowy figure silhouetted against a multitude of funeral pyres.

Immediately, I heard him say, "I was waiting for you." I told him, "Last evening, you disappeared in a flash. I looked around for you. All I could see were funeral pyres at this Gateway of Heaven, silent groups of men squatting around some pyres."

"Yes, I had to leave in a hurry. You see, I was getting angry at Jagannath as he was not answering my questions."

We chatted some more about his daily routine, my life in Chicago, a perfectly normal exchange though with an eerie background. Then, abruptly, there was silence and obviously, Mr. Panda had gone into a trance-like state and a resumption of the two-way dialogue, that is, between him and God.

"Your majestic presence on this coastal town, considered sacred by Hindus all over the world, no doubt, has given solace to millions who flock to your temple daily. Yet, you look around in Orissa and in fact, entire India. This society is now being run on lies and deceptions, and plunder of the state treasury. The country is on the verge of moral and economic collapse. India is facing an abyss. Your people need your re-incarnation of another Krishna in the battle field and new guidance to your people who do not even realize what they are facing." His voice was rising, increasingly accusatory in tone. As expected, there was a change of voice to the impersonated voice of the Lord of the World.

"Yes, I hear you. I will return as the Lord Shiva or Durga. I assure you I am Omnipotent, Omnipresent and Omniscient. The time is fast approaching when I will come and guide the people again. There will be a gigantic struggle, a war far exceeding the horrors of Mahabharata, a war within the minds of men and right will triumph."

Then, there was silence. Mr. Panda remained in a trance. After several minutes, a very sweet voice came through, "Dr. Sonjee, I will be proceeding to the Radhakanta Matha, the monastery where Sri Chaitanya used to stay. He came to Puri in 1510 AD and made this pilgrimage city the center of his religious mission and activity."

"Yes, I know about Chaitanya. I will come with you. I know where it is located. We will listen to the devotional Kirtans popularized by Chaitanya."

We walked together in silence and soon reached this monastery. We participated in the musical chanting of names of the Lord. Apparently, it goes on day and night. Finally, we parted company, he proceeding to his boarding house and I to my hotel. I asked him whether I would see him again next evening, but there was no response. When we were about to part company and in a gesture of friendship and warmth, he vigorously shook my hands and then started sobbing on my chest. Then, he was gone.

I stayed in Puri a few more days, walked on the beach every evening and regularly visited the cremation ground, looked for him in vain. Finally, one morning I went to his boarding house. I was told by the manager that Mr. Panda had not returned and it was his speculation that he might have gone to Balasore to visit with friends and relatives.

I was to depart from Bhubaneswar to Delhi on the evening flight and from there, proceed to New York. Puri was a bittersweet experience. I was not able to say good-bye to the man conversing with the Lord of the World, Jagannath in the cremation site, the Gateway to Heaven. I was just glancing through the morning paper when I noticed a brief news item indicating that the body of an elderly man, yet to be identified, had been recovered on the beach some seven miles from Puri. I was overcome with an intense feeling of horror. The report indicated that according to Police, it was a case of accidental drowning and no foul play was suspected. Autopsy was scheduled in the Puri Hospital.

Immediately, I took a taxi to the Puri Hospital and reported to the Police Officer who was in charge of the investigations. I was very agitated but the Officer was patient, listened to my story. He reported to me that there was no identification. In the meanwhile, I narrated to him my meetings with an elderly male in the cremation site and his conversation with Jagannath. The officer seemed curious but skeptical but assured me that I would be allowed to view the body as soon as the autopsy was finished.

After about an hour I was escorted to view the body and my heart sank. It was Mr. Panda. I related to the Officer that the deceased had been a recluse. He might have some relatives but had not maintained any contact with them. I requested the authorities to release the body to me and that I would take care of the funeral rites. I re-scheduled my flight from Bhubaneswar to Delhi. I was interviewed by police officers for hours. With my unbelievable story, they might have thought that here was another Oriya who had gone crazy in America. At the end of the day, the body was released to me for funeral rites. Three Police Officers came forward to assist me in making elaborate arrangements. It was just after sunset that the body was brought to the Gateway of Heaven cremation site. With all the appropriate rites and rituals, the body was ignited. I remembered Jagannath's voice coming via the departed that He would come to the earth and cleanse India and Orissa of all evils.

The Guru

It must have been mid-afternoon of a beautiful fall day in October when I had a phone call from Dr. Bose, an internist in Vancouver, British Columbia. He was a close friend of mine. I was a psychiatrist in that gem of a city, mainly engaged in forensic psychiatry. My friend had come to Canada many years back from Calcutta, India via England. He was a bit of an eccentric, but I loved him.

"Dr. Sonjee, will you be interested in coming with me tomorrow evening to listen to Guru Premananda? I understand he is going to talk about one of the Upanishads, specifically, Katha Upanishad, Death as Teacher. The event will be in the auditorium of the Mahalakshmi Hindu Temple on 11th Avenue East."

Dr. Bose was always inclined to listen to anyone who would come over from India and proclaim himself a wise Guru. I thought he was a bit naive and a simpleton.

"Dr. Bose, you know very well how I feel about these Gurus coming to North America in a steady stream. I am sorry I have no time for such activities. I realize there is a kind of existential and spiritual void in many people in North America. These Gurus are coming over to exploit the naive, both in U.S.A. and Canada."

"Dr. Sonjee, you psychiatrists are grandiose. You think you understand the human mind. This Guru is unlike the other Gurus who have come to Vancouver. He is charismatic, warm, friendly, handsome, a picture of health, a bachelor and above all, a great teacher."

I couldn't decline the invitation from my dear friend. I invited him to dinner in an Indian restaurant prior to the lecture at the Hindu Temple. During dinner, we talked mostly about his home city of Calcutta. His nostalgia for Calcutta was profound, pervasive and infectious. It was his beloved city. He knew all the historic antiquities of Calcutta. He could talk for hours on Calcutta of the eighteenth century, of Clive and Warren Hastings, the Governor General of India when the American colonies were engaged in the War of Independence against the British. My interest in the British history of Calcutta started in my high school days. Thus, we shared a deep love for the city and her people.

Dr. Bose had been visiting Calcutta regularly but would always return disgusted and disappointed. He never could realize that the Calcutta of his childhood was no more, and basically, he was now a foreigner in that city. Calcutta had just celebrated her tricentennial in 1990. Dr. Bose had kept in close touch, from distant Canada, with all the cultural events surrounding the celebration. I had listened to his endless discourses on Calcutta. I didn't have the heart to tell him that, in my view, he had no country of his own and that he was a foreigner both in Calcutta and Canada.

The lecture hall was full — mostly native Canadians, white folks but only a handful of South Asians. The Guruji, Swami Premananda, was certainly alive, vibrant, a picture of good health and with a sense of humor. He exuded warmth. His discussion on this very complex Katha Upanishad was analytical. He spoke for an hour or so. I was not bored. He had all the attributes of a great teacher, especially the ability to reach out.

My friend, Dr, Bose, was so moved that he was unable to discuss it, a departure from his usual behavior.

"Dr. Sonjee, what do you think?"

I simply responded, "I was quite impressed with his insightful and analytical interpretations of this highly complex Katha Upanishad, Death as Teacher."

Swami Premananda stayed on in Vancouver. He had attracted a large number of devotees, mostly white but of many professions. In addition to regular lectures, Swamiji started on individual spiritual counseling. He led a simple life. He had no desire for monetary gains. He didn't engage in any fund raising activities. He continued his selfless work without any expectations of praise or gratitude. Dr. Bose and I made a regular habit of having dinner in an Indian restaurant and attending Swamiji's lectures on various philosophies and scriptural teachings of Hinduism. He never put down the other great religions. He never suggested conversion to Hinduism.

Dr. Bose and I would occasionally see Swamiji in various Hindu festivals such as those celebrated in the Mahalakshmi Hindu Temple. On these special occasions, he radiated warmth and joy.

Swamiji had been now at Vancouver for a couple of years. He was immensely popular. Wherever he went in Vancouver, he was usually accompanied by a number of devotees, both male and female. These devotees had become his followers. Obviously he was contributing to the spiritual well-being of the people of Vancouver. Even politicians of British Columbia consulted with him.

Late one evening I received a call from Dr. Bose. He seemed anxious. He said, "Dr. Sonjee, I do not know what to make of this. I just do not believe it. It cannot be true. It is a part of a conspiracy to denigrate Swamiji. There may be jealousy." I interrupted him as he had not told me what it was all about. "Dr. Bose, what is it about Swamiji? Please calm down."

"Dr. Sonjee, I heard this terrible rumor from one of my patients today, that Swamiji has been having affairs with a number of his female devotees—not just one girl friend, but many. This rumor, according to my patient, was going around the circles of devotees, but surprisingly, nothing has changed on the surface."

I responded, "Dr. Bose, perhaps, some of his female devotees believe they are in love with him and that it is possible that these devotees' fantasies are running wild. Dr.Bose, let us go on a long walk tomorrow, Sunday, to Queen Elizabeth Park, and talk about this. I will pick you up around seven. We will have breakfast at the South Indian restaurant near the park and then go for a walk."

Next morning, during our walk, Dr. Bose added some more details of these rumors. He said, "Swamiji, according to my patient, has at least four girl friends: one, a Filipina called Marcella, a blond Helen, a Canadian; an English lady who arrived at Vancouver recently from Manchester, England; and a native of India, a lady known as Meena. The rumor is that some other devotees arrange these love trysts for Swamiji and that these sessions take place not in the temple complex, but adjoining buildings."

"Dr. Bose, how credible is your patient? There may not be a shred of evidence to all this. It is all in the fantasy land. You know, we psychiatrists have female patients who, during the course of therapy, fall in love, so to speak, with us. As soon as such material emerges during psychotherapy sessions, either through the patient's dreams, expression of fantasies or non- verbal behavior, the therapist must deal with it via interpretations, or face the risk of losing the patient. In psychoanalytic jargon these phenomena are called transference and counter-transference."

"But, Dr. Sonjee, I have difficulty in understanding what you are saying. Can you describe an example?"

"Yes, I will, from my own personal experience. Many, many years back, when I was training to be a psychiatrist, I was doing psychotherapy with a 27-year old single female school teacher. After many, many sessions, on one occasion she brought forth a dream of having inter-racial children. Immediately,

I recognized that she was falling in love with me, so to speak. On an intellectual level, I knew I should deal with it and clarify our professional relationship, but I didn't. Perhaps I was attracted to her. You know, she was single and I, too. In fact, I am sure I was quite attracted towards her because I would be anticipating her coming to the session."

"Dr. Sonjee, do you mean that you were having fantasies of having sex with her?"

"I wouldn't put it that explicitly. Shall we say, I was physically attracted towards her. I sought out my supervisor, a reputed psychoanalyst, trained by Anna Freud, daughter of the great Sigmund Freud himself. He told me that as a physician, I mismanaged the situation and that I should have dealt with that sexually-oriented material immediately, for the benefit of the patient. He predicted that the patient wouldn't return to me. I thought he was bluffing but you know, he was right. That patient canceled out with me. I still feel badly over it."

"Dr. Sonjee, let us come back to the Guru Premananda. I can probably understand his having an affair with only one seductive, beautiful female but four or five females? That is beyond me."

"Dr. Bose, man biologically is not monogamous. But let us talk about what we should do."

"Dr. Sonjee, let me talk with my patient some more, to find out some more details. I am really distressed. If true, it will be a big disgrace to the Indian community of Vancouver. It will give India a bad name."

"Dr. Bose, let us not be carried away. This has nothing to do with India or her ancient civilization. We are talking about one wise man who might have fallen into temptations."

Dr. Bose and I kept in touch with each other, even continued to attend Swamiji's lectures.

It was sometime in the spring of 1993 that the daily newspaper, Vancouver Sun, published a piece of news that was staggering. I read it again and again, just to be sure I was reading it right. I could hardly believe what I read. It was something about a Guru from India, Swami Premananda, being arrested on a charge of rape. He had been remanded to judicial custody but bailed out by devotees. The news item mentioned that one of his devotees, Florence Robinson, had filed the charge against him. I was stunned. I called Dr. Bose immediately, "Dr. Bose, have you read today's Vancouver Sun?"

"Dr. Sonjee, no, I haven't read it, but one of my patients told me about Swamiji being arrested and remanded to judicial custody and then bailed. Let us have dinner this evening and talk about it."

Dr. Bose had more information about the alleged rape.,"Apparently Ms. Robinson, being married, had pangs of guilt and had wanted to cut off the relationship with the Guru. She had gone to his room to inform him about it and that is where the rape happened. Many devotees believe that Ms. Robinson set a trap for the Guru and that she is being blamed for alternating between seducing and rejecting the Guru. It is being investigated by the RCMP. It may come to a trial, a very unpleasant thing to think about."

I was genuinely fond of the Guru. I admired him for his spiritual insight, warm personality and his ability to respond to the deep emotional needs of his devotees thru his counseling and talks. I was tempted to have a talk with Guru Premananda but decided against it. On the surface, the Guru continued his lectures. He never referred to the charges against him and many of his devotees remained fiercely loyal. However, there was a drop in attendance at his meetings. No member of the Hindu community in Vancouver came forth to support him. For many months, the investigations continued. Dr. Bose and I heard rumors that many of his devotees had been interrogated and that reportedly at least five other women had alleged inappropriate sexual behavior by the Guru towards them, and that they were willing to testify. We also heard that two prominent attorneys were defending Swamiji. Neither Dr. Bose nor I wanted to see the spectacle of the Guru put on trial. We were afraid that the media would have a field day reporting testimony of the various witnesses, and that indirectly, the prosecution would put even Hinduism and India on trial.

One afternoon in my office I had a call from one Mr. James who introduced himself as an attorney defending the Guru and wishing to set up an appointment to see me in regard to the case. I reluctantly agreed to this request. I was doing exclusively forensic psychiatry in Vancouver and Victoria and I didn't wish to be involved in this particular situation. I had heard about Mr. James as a prominent and competent defense attorney in British Columbia. We agreed that he would come to my office the next day. Mr. James was one of those sophisticated, smooth, personable and, above all, a very clever attorney. Briefly, he requested me to do a psychiatric evaluation on Guru Premananda as he was going to introduce psychiatric expert testimony in the trial.

I responded, "Mr. James, you understand that I admire the Guruji immensely. There is no way I can be objective and my opinion, whatever it might be, would be subjected to cruel cross examination by the prosecution, especially because I am a Hindu from India."

He was not a person to easily convince and he replied, "You are the person I want as a psychiatrist for the defense. Your specialty is forensic psychiatry and you are a Hindu from India. You are the right person to explain the complexity of Guruji's behavior to the jury." I continued to decline and finally, he gave up and said, "Perhaps I can convince the Court to bring you in as an amicus curiae, that is, a friend of the Court."

Dr. Bose and I met frequently. The upcoming trial made both of us anxious. I made many evening visits to the Library of the College of Law of the University of British Columbia to research materials and case laws in regard to my testimony as a friend of the Court.

The trial was highly publicized in the media. The Indian community in Vancouver and as a matter of fact, in entire Canada seemed to be the focus of various media coverage. The learned Hindu Guru was being tried on the media before the trial.

The trial began with jury selection. Anyone with a bias against Hindus was eliminated. At least, five females testified against the Guru. They were subjected to severe cross examination by the defense team of lawyers headed by Mr. James. Florence Robinson, who had pressed the rape charge against the Guru, maintained her poise during the cross-examination. She stuck to her story, that she was a devotee of Guruji and that due to personal crisis, she had several sessions of individual counseling with Guru. She described the attempted rape scene without showing much emotion. She consistently denied any seductive behavior in these sessions with the Guru. Part of that cross examination was as follows:

Mr. James: "Ms. Robinson, was there anything in your behavior that would arouse a man? I mean, seduction, flirting and other non-verbal cues that might arouse a man?" Ms. Robinson, a quite attractive blond of English background responded, "Mr. James, I was in a state of depression due to a personal crisis in my family. I had attended many sessions of lectures and discussions by Guruji and I had a fascination with Hindu philosophy as propounded by Guruji, and I was most sincere in getting help from him. No, to your question, I do not believe I exhibited such behavior as you mention. Let me add, I didn't have any sexual fantasies about Guruji."

Ms. Robinson had described in details as to how unexpectedly during one of these sessions, Guruji tried to make love to her and finally forced himself on her despite her resistance. Only at this point she sobbed quietly.

A number of previous devotees also testified against the Guru, on various behaviors that would be sexual harassment. I had been allowed to attend each session as my upcoming testimony was simply to assist the Court. Finally, I had my day in Court.

Mr. James, leading the team of defense lawyers, took several minutes in establishing my credentials as a forensic psychiatrist. He also established the fact that I had some knowledge of Hindu scriptures and that I had no personal friendship with Guru Premananda.

Mr. James, "Dr. Sonjee, you have listened to all the testimony in this court for the last several days. Can you please give your opinion as a psychiatrist and in order to advise the Court? My client is likely to face twenty years in prison if he is found guilty. I do not deny that evidence is stacked against my client. In fact, in the media, he has been found guilty even prior to the trial. I understand you had attended many lecture and discussion sessions by the Guru. Let me ask you a bit more about your background. Are you a practicing Hindu?"

I responded, "Yes, Mr. James, I remain a Hindu. Of course, in Vancouver, we do not carry on all the rituals and ceremonies that Hindu families normally do in India."

I had learned in my forensic psychiatric career that an expert should be brief and responsive, and always maintain proper decorum and respect for the Court.

"Dr. Sonjee, are you aware that Guru Premananda, in his discourses and talks at Vancouver, has been able to rekindle a spiritual awakening in thousands of people? Are you aware that many eminent professionals in law, medicine, government, business, and teaching have been ardent followers of Guruji?"

Immediately, the prosecution objected claiming such questions have no relevance to the criminal trial.

The Judge firmly stated, "Objection over-ruled. Dr. Sonjee, please answer the question."

My brief response to Mr. James was, "Yes". Mr. James looked at the jury and proceeded, "As a psychiatrist, can you be objective and present to the Court a clinical, scientific opinion? Our position is that any sexual relationships between my client and the accusers was consensual. It was a mutually agreed expression of behavior. The prosecution has not presented any evidence that these women were not competent. Perhaps, these women were needy, perhaps compassion and warmth, as expressed by my client, were misinterpreted by these women as seduction or perhaps, my client shouldn't have engaged in such relationships. But the bottom line is that it was consensual. My client has consistently denied any force whatsoever. Dr. Sonjee, I now ask you to give your opinion and advise the Court and the jury."

I had fully prepared my testimony. I made eye contact with the Judge and the Jury and proceeded as follows: "Mr. James, Swami Premananda is a profound scholar, a spiritual counselor. He is warm, compassionate and charismatic. But, let us not forget that he is a man in the prime of his youth and that he comes from a sexually inhibitive, restrictive and cloistered society of India. In other words, he comes from a society which practices sexual repression."

Mr. James interrupted, "Dr. Sonjee, I ask you to explain yourself more fully. You might be talking about cultural misunderstandings in this particular situation."

"Precisely. The Guru probably misunderstood his female devotees. These women were outgoing, warm and friendly. They are beautiful, not necessarily seductive, but perhaps both parties had sexual fantasies about the other."

"Dr. Sonjee, do you have a psychiatric diagnosis on the Guru? Do you think he has any mental or personality disorder?"

"Mr. James, I have not examined the Guru and therefore, it will be most inappropriate for me to even speculate on diagnosis. However, I can say that it is normal for men to have sexual fantasies. It is a sort of safety valve. In this particular situation, it led to consensual sex."

At this point, the prosecution objected thus: "Your Honor, I object. Dr. Sonjee refers to consensual sex, but it has been clearly established that it was rape."

The Judge stated, "Objection sustained. Dr. Sonjee, you should confine your opinions to matters related to psychiatry and interpretation of the Hindu culture. Mr. James, please proceed."

"Dr. Sonjee, do you have an opinion as to the disposition of this case? As an amicus curiae, I am asking you to give your opinion as to what will serve the purpose of justice."

The prosecution again objected but was over-ruled by the judge, who stated, "Dr. Sonjee, whether it was consensual sex, or sexual harassment, or a misdemeanor, or even innocence, the Jury and the Court will decide. But please proceed with your opinion in response to Mr. James' question."

My opinion was as follows, "Your Honor, a person given the trust of his or her client must not violate it. The Guru, even if it was consensual sex violated the trust. That counseling relationship became sexualized."

Mr. James interrupted, "Dr. Sonjee, can you please give an example? Do you have an episode from your own experiences as a psychiatrist?"

I was not prepared for this and I looked at the Judge for help. The Honorable Judge got the hint and stated, "Proceed with an example or two from your own experiences as a psychiatrist."

"Your Honor, I will comply with your order, but, for the sake of confidentiality, I will not divulge dates, names and places, etc., and will simply give situations with some patients of the opposite sex, who were in psychotherapy with me. I will give only two examples. First, there was an attractive woman of 27 who had neurotic symptoms of various kinds and was improving. She had a good rapport with me as her therapist. On one occasion, she brought a dream of inter-racial children. She was a white female and I, from India. This dream was a manifestation of the therapeutic relationship that was getting sexualized. It was like a red flag, and I should have dealt with it immediately, that is, interpreted to her and clarified the business nature of the relationship but I didn't. Obviously, she had sexual fantasies about me."

"Dr. Sonjee, " Mr. James interrupted, "We are lay people. Please clarify to the Court as to why you didn't do what you say you should have done."

"I didn't help her understand what was going on because of my own attraction towards her."

"Did you have sexual fantasies about her?"

"I hate to admit it but I had. In this situation the patient quit treatment. In the case of Guru's counseling with his female devotees, such situations probably escalated to what happened between them, that is, a therapeutic relationship gradually deteriorating into a sexual relationship."

The Judge said, "Dr. Sonjee, do you have another example?"

"Yes, your Honor, in this instance, a female patient of mine had improved greatly from panic attacks and social phobia. She was a married professional woman. One evening, I had a call from this young lady inviting me to a cocktail in a hotel. She was quite seductive in her voice. Was I tempted to go over? No, I was polite and firm and encouraged her to go home, and explained to her that my relationship with her was only professional."

Mr. James then proceeded, "Dr. Sonjee, do you have an opinion as to the disposition of this case?"

At this point, I requested the Court for a recess, which was granted. During the recess, I and Dr. Bose went out of the building for a consultation. It seemed my friend, Dr. Bose, was angry. He didn't think my testimony was strong enough to protect the Guru. He said, "Dr. Sonjee, you spoke of violation of trust. If the Guru is convicted, the entire Indian community in Vancouver will be put to shame. People of

Vancouver will mock at Hinduism. I am really disappointed." Then he left abruptly in great haste. On resumption, the Judge disallowed any testimony from me on disposition. It was then the turn of the prosecution to cross-examine me. Essentially, my testimony didn't change significantly. I was dismissed as a witness.

To my utter surprise, Mr. James requested the Judge to put another witness under oath and he mentioned, "Dr. Bose, a prominent internist of Vancouver and a devotee of Swami Premananda."

After he was sworn in, Mr. James asked Dr. Bose thus, "Dr. Bose, you have volunteered to testify. You have admitted to me that you admire Swami Premananda very much. You also feel that Swamiji has contributed a lot to the people of Vancouver. Please make your statement."

Dr. Bose stated thus, "Your Honor, Members of the Jury, I plead with you to balance justice with compassion and consider Guruji's immense contributions to spiritual living and happiness in this beautiful city of Vancouver. We Hindus are raised in a sexually repressive society."

At this point, much to my embarrassment, Dr. Bose went into a rambling talk on Hindu scriptures, the Gita, the Upanishads and as to how the Guru was filling a spiritual and existential void in Vancouver.

Obviously, both Mr. James, the prosecution counsel and the Judge were getting fidgety. Mr. James intervened at this point, "Dr. Bose, do you have a recommendation?"

"Yes, Mr. James, if the Guruji is found guilty, he should be placed on probation. If supervision is required as a condition of probation, then, I am offering myself as a person who is willing to take that role. If the Court finds the Guruji needs a psychiatrist to supervise him and give him guidance and counseling, there is a man here in the courtroom who can do it." He pointed his finger at me. "I further suggest that as a condition of probation, Guru Premananda be required to go door to door, on a planned and regular basis, to offer spiritual counseling."

The Judge intervened at this point, "Dr. Bose, are you suggesting that the accused go door to door to preach an alien religion such as Hinduism?"

"No, your Honor, nothing like that. We are stepping into the twenty-first century. It is time for ministers, gurus, priests and swamis to come out of their cloistered places and go out to the streets and people's homes to engage them in spiritual counseling and guide them. It has nothing to do with preaching Hinduism. Of course, in this particular instance, the Guruji will bring the ancient wisdom of Hinduism."

Both the prosecution and the defense rested their cases. The Court was adjourned. Mr. James and Guru Premananda came over first to Dr. Bose and then, to me. We hugged each other. The Guru broke down and started sobbing on the chest of Dr. Bose.

MY DEAR COLONEL RUSSELL

It was the summer of 1981 when I was in London to attend the World Congress of Psychiatry. I had been in the private practice of psychiatry in Philadelphia for a number of years. I loved the City of Brotherly Love.

However underneath this facade of brotherly love, many African-American neighborhoods were seething with anger, despair and hopelessness. It was not surprising that at times this city would explode with racial riots.

I genuinely loved my African-American friends. Once they could shed their racial paranoia and got to know you, generally they were warm, friendly and with a ready and hearty laughter. In the World Congress of Psychiatry, I was due to present a paper on 'Psychiatric Aspects of Racial Discrimination in America'. Also, I looked forward to visit the great museums and historical sites of London. Having been born a citizen of British India, I have had this love-hate relationship with the British.

It was a beautiful Sunday afternoon when I headed towards the Tower of London. This important monument on the River Thames had witnessed much of British history. It was the royal residence until the reign of James I. And James I was the King who sent an Ambassador to the Court of Emperor Jahangir. I was particularly interested in an area called Tower Green where Henry VIII had ordered two of his wives, Anne Boleyn and Catherine Howard, to be executed. It should be mentioned here that Anne Boleyn was the mother of Queen Elizabeth I, who signed the charter of the East India Company in 1600 and this company eventually laid the foundation of their Empire in India. I was listening to the Tower guide about Henry VIII and his wives and the details of the execution. The description was so vivid and gruesome that I could visualize the entire scene in front of me and what took place in 1536. I felt a bit sick in my stomach and almost without thinking, I said a prayer to our Hindu God Jagannath of Puri, for the departed soul of Anne Boleyn. I also felt foolish in realizing that here I was a Hindu praying for the soul of an English Queen who was executed on the orders of her husband more than four hundred years back.

I was about to follow the guide, along with the group, to the next historical site, when I felt a gentle tap on my right shoulder. I turned around and saw an elderly gentleman, who softly said, "I am sorry. I hope you didn't mind but are you from India?" I shook his hands and introduced myself, "Yes, I am Dr. Sonjee. I am originally from India." With that I was about to give him the brush-off and get on with the tour, but there was something about the frail, elderly Englishman, something in his facial expression and his eyes that touched me. I continued, "I am now a doctor in America, in the city of Philadelphia and I am attending the World Congress of Psychiatry here in London." He shook my hands again and said, "I am Col. Russell. Where are you from in India?" The tour group was moving away and I was anxious not to miss it, but wished not to be rude.

"Col. Russell, originally, I am from a very small town called Sambalpur in the north-western part of Orissa." With that I started moving away from him, when Col. Russell literally stood in my way and said, "Dr. Sonjee, I will be delighted if you please join me for a cup of tea after we finish the tour."

"Yes, it will be a pleasure."

During tea at the canteen, we talked small things. He had indicated that he had served in India in the late 1930's. He said, "Dr. Sonjee, if you are free this evening, I would very much like you to come to my apartment. You know, I miss India even after so many years." I accepted his invitation. I thought, this old British fellow would like to share some of his tales of the Raj and I have had a special fondness for those stories. On the way to his home in the bus, we chatted about the current situation in India. He seemed to be in his late 70's or early 80's but in apparent good health. Throughout the bus ride, he had many questions about both the town and the district of Sambalpur.

His apartment was elegantly furnished, cozy and comfortable. He said that he had remained single. There were various paintings of Indian scenes and Indian artifacts throughout the place.

"Dr. Sonjee, I am going to fix myself a Scotch. Would you like to have one?"

"No, thank you very much Col. Russell." I got up and looked at some of the paintings. One drew my attention and I read the caption, "Col. Gilbert's Residence, Sambalpur, 1828." It was a colonial residence obviously on the River Mahanadi. "Dr. Sonjee, that is a reproduction of an original painting in the India Office Records and Library here in London."

He settled down in a comfortable chair. "I will fix some vegetable curry and a fish soup such as made in Sambalpur and rice. " I was getting a bit hungry and offered to help him out in the kitchen. While busy in the kitchen, we kept chatting about Orissa. He mentioned that Sir John Hubback was the first Governor of Orissa, in 1936, when it became a separate British Province.

"Dr. Sonjee, tell me about you Sital Sasthi Festival. It was some sort of a marriage ritual of one of your Gods. Wasn't it?"

"Yes, it is the marriage festival of God Shiva and Parvati. In the eyes of a child in Sambalpur, I can tell you, Col. Russell, it was a wonderful festival."

"Dr. Sonjee, I thought, you people were nuts to celebrate something like that, but even as an Englishman, I enjoyed the gaiety and festivity of your people. Should I admit to you now that when I passed your God Shiva in his chariot, I offered a salute?"

I laughed and said, "Col. Russell, you were District Superintendent of Police and you a Christian, saluted our Lord Shiva?"

"Dr. Sonjee, I could only hope that none of my men would report me to the Governor's Office at Cuttack."

Both of us laughed.

Surprisingly, he prepared an excellent dinner. We chatted amicably during our meal, mostly about Sambalpur and the festivals. When he had brought out dessert, he said in a somber voice, "Do you have time to listen to my story?"

"Yes, Col. Russell, I was waiting for this moment." I looked at my watch. It was past eight in the evening. I will relate his story mostly in his own words. He proceeded, "Dr. Sonjee, do you know why I tapped on your shoulder in the Tower of London? You looked like a typical man from the Sambalpur region of Orissa. I had that inexplicable feeling that here was a fellow who might be from western Orissa and I must take the chance."

"Col. Russell, you must have experienced some extra-sensory perception but please proceed with your story."

"Dr. Sonjee, I think, on the bus ride, you told me you were a psychiatrist. You might think, I am insane."

"You need not worry Col. Russell, there is a core of insanity in everyone."

"You remember, Dr. Sonjee, I told you that I was the District Superintendent of Police for three years in Sambalpur between 1938 and 1941. You remember the road to the Court and the residence of the Deputy Commissioner, close to the bank of your Mahanadi River. My official bungalow was just across the residence of the Deputy Commissioner. I came out to India as a young man. I was born in 1904 in Lincoln, England. My family had a tradition of service in India. Two of my uncles served in the Calcutta Police Force. One of my great uncles on the maternal side was killed in Cawnpore during the Sepoy Mutiny of 1857. It was a formidable job, to be in charge of police administration of such a huge district. I can tell you true stories of all kinds of police encounters, but such can wait. Let me refresh my drink. Yes, Dr. Sonjee, have you been lonely, I mean that sense of loneliness, homesickness, feeling not wanted or needed, a sort of estrangement or perhaps, depression and specially, in a foreign country? When you went to America, you might have experienced what I am talking about."

"Col. Russell, how right you are. It was not only loneliness but bouts of depression and guilt for leaving India and mourning for people close to my heart. You remember the Hindu cremation site in front of Pataneswari Temple and the river bank of Sambalpur. My heart cringes with pain, when imagined scenes of the cremation site intrude on my memory but Col. Russell, please proceed with your story."

"Dr. Sonjee, I remember that Hindu cremation site. I am sorry, if I aroused painful memories. Let me return to my story. In Sambalpur, I had a number of servants including a young girl of about seventeen. You know about the tribal people of your district, simple, honest, trusting, warm and quite beautiful. This young lady, a converted Christian, knew a smattering of English. I have a photograph of her. Let me show it to you."

With that Col. Russell went to his bedroom and returned with a tattered photograph. He gingerly handed it over to me. I could very easily make out a beautiful young lady in tribal jewelry of Sambalpur with an enchanting smile. The background was that of a garden. I was still engrossed looking at this photograph when I heard faint sobbing. I went over to Col. Russell, hugged him.

"Col. Russell, will it help you to relate to me the entire story?"

He resumed his story, "Priya, that is her name, was so outgoing and open, and with her broken English and peals of laughter, she brought something to me that, at first, I had difficulty in understanding. Mind you, she was not seductive. Dr. Sonjee, do you understand what I am talking about? She was utterly child-like, so open, so trusting. Falling in love with her does not quite describe what happened. You can imagine in those days, a young English officer having a relationship with a tribal girl of Sambalpur."

"Col. Russell, I can understand. In my college days, my friends and I used to visit villages on the occasion of Hindu festivals. Once under a full moon, I watched a folk dance of tribal women. We could barely make out the figures of these women dancing and singing to some old folk tales of Sambalpur. If I were you, I too would have had a relationship with Priya."

"Yes, Dr. Sonjee, you are so understanding. You might have gone thru similar situations in life. Yes, we had a relationship for almost a year. Priya became pregnant. You know very well how gossipy people in Sambalpur can be. Finally, it reached the ears of the Deputy Commissioner. I was called to the carpet. He was my boss. I remember the scene very well. He was enraged. He started screaming at me, accusing me of having an affair with a 'nigger' and having brought down British prestige in Sambalpur. I listened quietly. I feared he might lunge at me. He was frothing at the corners of his mouth. At times, he would strike his fist on his desk. He said he was ashamed of me. His ravings and rantings went on and on for what seemed like an eternity. Then, there was a pause. He wiped his forehead, got up from his chair, came over to me and shook my hand."

He said, "Being a Civil Servant in Imperial India has taken the humanity out of me. We, the Britishers, have dehumanized the people of India, but in the process, we have dehumanized ourselves. I had almost forgotten I was dealing with human beings."

He returned to his chair and asked me to sit down and ordered tea. I didn't know what to expect. He seemed to be struggling with himself, anxious and perspiring. We sipped tea in silence. Then, as if in an impulse, he reached out to the bottom of a drawer on his desk, to take out an old envelope and pulled out a photograph. Soon, he came over to me, put his arm around me and showed me the photograph. It was quite faded, but a picture of a beautiful young lady in Punjabi costume. Below, it was simply written, 'Lahore, 1910'.

I was speechless for a moment, but then, I could only mutter, 'Sir, Sir'. He took the photograph looked at it again, gently and gingerly put it back. He took his time, sipping tea and said, 'She was a Punjabi girl'. Then, abruptly, he announced, 'Col. Russell, I will recommend your transfer to another Province, far away from Sambalpur.' Being a faithful and loyal officer, I didn't protest.

I made an attempt to speak, but I was tongue-tied. He seemed to understand. He added that the Government of Orissa would be setting up a monthly grant to the girl and the unborn child. Only at that point, I protested and requested the Deputy Commissioner to allow me to stay in Sambalpur until the baby was born. My eyes were misty and my voice choked. Something must have touched my boss. He got up abruptly from his chair, went out to the window and I saw him wiping his eyes."

"Col. Russell, can you please fix me a Scotch?"

"Yes, Dr. Sonjee, I will fix you one and I will get a refill." He returned with two drinks. Then, he resumed, "'Dr. Sonjee, what my boss told me was touching, haunting. Let me tell you more or less in his own words, 'Col. Russell, in all confidentiality, I will tell you a bit more about this Hindu girl in Punjab. It was about 1910. I was, as you are now, fairly new in India. Her name was Sita. I too had a relationship with her. One evening she was lying on my chest in the back of our garden in my Lahore bungalow. She softly whispered that she had my baby. I remember, I was stunned. After several weeks, one night I asked her to return to her village to get an abortion. She flew into a rage. The next day she was gone. I asked and received a transfer to Orissa.' Then, he said that he was going to allow me to continue on my duties at Sambalpur until the baby was born but that Priya had to go to Jharsuguda to give birth. 'I will be at Cuttack in a few days on official business. I will make a trip to No. 8 Cantonment Road, residence of the Chief Secretary, to have a quiet word with him about you. It will be confidential.' I thanked him and left."

"Col. Russell, before you proceed with your story, please tell me what happened to the Deputy Commissioner."

"Dr. Sonjee, you remember the Quit India movement started by your Gandhi in August 1942. Mr. Moore was at that time posted in Koraput District of Orissa. Because of Gandhi's movement, vast areas of that district had erupted into rebellion against British rule. He had to take stern measures against unarmed villagers to suppress riots and rebellion. He died presumably of a heart attack in one of these trips to the interior of that district. Dr. Sonjee, let me return to my story. I stayed in Sambalpur. Priya had gone to Jharsuguda about thirty miles from Sambalpur. I kept in touch with her. Finally, I received the news that she had given birth to a baby boy.

I decided to go to Jharsuguda on an official visit but really to see Priya and my boy."

At this point, Col. Russell broke down. He started sobbing. I hugged him, patted him on the back. I suggested to Col. Russell that we should walk over to the nearby Indian Restaurant, The Taj India, for snacks. He readily agreed.

We ordered some delicious South India snacks. Col. Russell was well known to the restaurant staff as apparently, he was a regular visitor. Col. Russell kept talking about his days in Sambalpur, dishes his chef used to prepare and his activities in the Mahanadi Club of Sambalpur. During this talk of days gone bye, he confided that even in those days, when the World War II had started, he knew that the British Raj in India was going to end.

Col. Russell and I had another drink of Scotch and he resumed his story.

"Dr. Sonjee, do you remember how beautiful an early winter morning in your district is? I think, it was December that I started for Jharsuguda early one morning. I was going to see Priya and my son. Priya lived with her parents in the Christian section of Jharsuguda. I was not expecting any difficulties with the local population. You people of India are so accepting of others. Of course, I was the Police boss of the entire district. My Indian subordinates escorted me to Priya's house. With me, there were Mr. Das, Sub-Inspector of Police and three police-men. When we reached Priya's house, there was a fairly large gathering outside. I knew it was a friendly gathering. Mr. Das made way for me and I was inside the house. First I greeted Priya's parents and then, I went to Priya. I sat down by her and asked her to let me hold our son. He was only a couple of weeks old. I asked Priya whether she had named the baby and she just smiled and said 'no'. I then announced that the boy's name would be Mohan. I held my son in my arms for a long time. There was a joyous crowd around. Mr. Das stayed close to me. I knew, he was a devout Hindu, but he was so overwhelmed that he asked me if he could hold the baby. I handed over my son to him and he went over to Priya and said, 'Madam, after the Sahib leaves Sambalpur, I will look after you and Mohan.' I was so moved and happy that I started singing and doing an English jig."

"Col. Russell, Priya knew that you were leaving her. Did she say anything to you?" That seemed to jolt him. However, he said, Priya assured him that she was going to raise Mohan and he need not worry.

He resumed, "Priya's parents asked that I have lunch with them. You know, in those days, it was taboo for an Englishman to eat in an Indian's home. I decided that I would be a human being and agreed. I sat on the floor, cross-legged Indian style. Soon, it was time to leave and I planted a kiss on my baby, Mohan, but I couldn't do that to Priya. I went up to her and handed over our baby and simply said, 'God be with you.' I left my heart in that house."

Col. Russell started sobbing again. I was not able to console him. I just waited. He went for another drink.

"Dr. Sonjee, I returned to Sambalpur the same day. I had an order transferring me to Amritsar in Punjab. I saw my boss, the Deputy Commissioner, Mr. Moore. He told me I would be leaving for Amritsar in a week or so. He had me sit down and describe to him in all details my visit to Jharsuguda.

He listened with rapt attention, shook my hand and said, 'We the British will be humane only after our Empire is history!' I knew he was thinking of Sita in Punjab."

"Col. Russell, you could have married Priya and taken her and Mohan to Punjab with you."

"Dr. Sonjee, you are a psychiatrist. Don't you understand? We the British for two hundred years had built a barrier between your people and us that I was unable to surmount."

It was getting close to midnight.

"Dr. Sonjee, it is getting late. Let me finish. I want you to go to Jharsuguda on your next trip to India and look for Priya and Mohan. You see, after I left Orissa for Punjab, I got busy in my work. You know what Punjab was going through. I just didn't think about my son and Priya. I drank a lot every evening but was able to do my job. I was a witness to the 1947 massacres in Punjab. I left India in December 1947 and retired here in London. I would like you to inquire about my son and Priya and report to me."

I asked Col. Russell as to why he himself had not made the trip to Jharsuguda. He simply stated that many times he thought of making the trip but something prevented him from doing so. I assured him that I would go to Jharsuguda, make the inquiries and write to him.

It was about the fall of 1983 that I went to India. On my visit to Sambalpur, I told my family members that I was going to Jharsuguda for a day. I didn't tell anyone why I was going.

In Jharsuguda I decided to go to the Police station for help. I told one Officer Sahu the whole story.

Of course, none of them had heard of Col. Russell, but Mr. Sahu was gracious enough to accompany me to the Christian section of Jharsuguda. We went in a Police jeep. It was a Sunday and the morning services at the local Church was going on. Mr. Sahu had suggested that we stand outside the Church and ask people coming out of the Church if anyone re-called one Priya, a Christian girl, who had a baby by one Col. Russell and who was District Superin-tendent of Police some forty-four years back. Mr. Sahu posed this question repeatedly as I stood be-hind him. People did not respond and others were surprised at the question. Some greeted Mr. Sahu warmly but denied any knowledge of Priya. I knew it would be a miracle if someone in this small Chris-tian community would recall something like this after almost half-a-century. In a way, I was feeling relieved. But an elderly female, on being asked the same question, stopped for a moment and had Mr. Sahu repeat what he was asking about. I saw the old woman collapse in the arms of Mr. Sahu. There was a general commotion and I sprang up to assist Mr. Sahu. She was revived quickly and murmured, ' I am Priya's aunt. Dr. Sonjee, please come to my home for lunch.'

Mr. Sahu and I escorted her in the jeep and took her to her house. She introduced herself as Mrs. Mahanti. On reaching her home, we were seated while she fixed a delicious lunch, those heavenly Sambalpuri dishes. I decided to wait for her to tell the story of Mohan and Priya.

She first apologized for losing control of herself in the Church. She said, 'I never entertained in my wildest fantasies that this story about Col. Russell would resurface.' I briefly explained to her my encounter with Col. Russell about two years back in London and his assignment to me.

Mrs. Mahanti composed herself and gave the following story: 'Priya died at the age of 27 of typhoid. She took good care of her son, Mohan who was then about 10. Priya's parents took over the responsibility. Mohan seemed to do well. You know, he was a so-called Anglo-Indian, son of an Indian mother and English father. Mohan came to me many times to talk about his confusion as to who he was. Of course, after the death of his mother, it became more acute. He was in turmoil. He must have been around sixteen. Was it 1954? I guess, it was. One day he just left Jharsuguda. Just like that he was gone, no note, nothing. Even today, we do not know. He could have gone to England to search for his father. He could have gone to Australia. It is almost thirty years now, we have heard nothing. He just was gone. Priya's parents were beyond consolation. Both of them had raised Mohan as their own son. Soon after, they passed away. What else can I tell you?'

I had no heart to quiz her anymore. I was stunned. I wished I had not made this trip to Jharsuguda. We sat in silence. I asked Mrs. Mahanti where Priya was buried. She said that she was buried in the Christian cemetery. She offered to accompany me there if I wished to visit her grave. It was late afternoon. Mr. Sahu, I and Mrs. Mahanti were on our way to visit the cemetery and on reaching it, she guided us to the grave of Priya. I stood by the grave with folded hands and said loudly, 'Priya, Priya, if you can hear me, Col. Russell has a message for you, that is, even now after forty five years, his heart carries your love for him and his pain for separation from his son, Mohan. I touched the grave tenderly and put one single red rose which Mr. Sahu handed over to me. I stood there in prayerful silence. Then, I turned around and saw the big burly Police Officer, Mr. Sahu, sobbing silently, two Hindus at the grave site of a Christian girl who had passed away many many years back.

I stayed in Sambalpur for two more weeks. However, Col. Russell was always in my mind. What to tell him and what not to. I was literally torn apart. Then, a thought came to me that I should visit our Goddess Samaleswari in Sambalpur and pray her for guidance. Just prior to departure from Sambalpur and on my way back to America, I found a day that I could visit the temple and pray to her for guidance on that matter. I visited the inner sanctum and prayed to Goddess Samaleswari for guidance. I was keenly aware that many of my forefathers came to the same sanctum and had prayed to the Goddess for guidance. At the moment, no guidance came from the Goddess.

I returned to my home in Philadelphia. That encounter with Col. Russell was like a bad dream. It was no longer in my mind. Then, one night I had a dream as to what to write to Col. Russell. It was like a nightmare. The language was so clear that I woke up, in perspiration and wrote it down lest it would evaporate. I sent the following letter to Col. Russell:

December 3, 1983

3139 Crawford Street
Philadelphia, Pennsylvania
USA 19129

Col. James Russell
203 Blackfriars Road, Apartment No. 7
London SE1 8NG
United Kingdom

Dear Col. Russell,

I hope this letter greets you in good health. You remember the assignment you gave me. It turned out to be not that simple. You remember, during your stay in Sambalpur the temple of Goddess Samaleswari in the old part of Sambalpur. What to write to you was so excruciatingly complex that I had to consult with our Goddess. I went to the inner sanctum of the temple and with folded hands, I briefly told our Goddess your story. I prayed her to give me guidance. I waited in vain and I returned disappointed. There was no word of guidance from our Goddess. Then, several days later, I had the dream and in which, Goddess conveyed to me what to write to you, and it is the following, 'Dear Col. Russell, Priya is in Peace and Mohan, your son, is somewhere. Lord Krishna in the Bhagavad Gita says to Arjuna 'The wise grieve neither for the living nor for the dead'. Dear Col. Russell, was it strange that our meeting took place in the Tower of London? Being a Hindu, I think, that meeting was ordained by our Goddess of Sambalpur.

With best wishes, I remain,

Sincerely Yours,

Dr. Sonjee

MY FRIEND FROM GERMANY

From where I lay, on the fifth floor of the Brooklyn Hospital, I could see the Statue of Liberty in the distance and the New York harbor. It was exactly forty years back that I had come to Pier 38 where the S. S. United States had docked after completing her maiden voyage from Southampton to New York. I distinctly remembered going through Immigration and Customs, on Ellis Island. I was the first person from India who had come on this historic voyage, on the new "Queen of the Atlantic." I still have the original dinner menu dated July 12, 1952. 1 could recall some passengers, an American novelist and an African-American couple, both social workers. I still had the passenger list of the voyage with me, a memento of my journey. There was a knock on the door.

"Dr. Sonjee, how are you? In our neighborhood newspaper, I read about you being injured in a car accident yesterday."

For a moment, I couldn't place him. Here was a man, mildly obese, partially bald, neatly dressed and with a warm and friendly expression.

"I am Peter Stein. Do you recall I came to you for consultation about twenty years ago? You and I were passengers on the S. S. United States in 1952."

I stretched out my hands, greeted him, even managing a smile. I remembered that Peter had escaped from Nazi Germany in 1937 when he was about 12. His parents had sent him to England to join an uncle and aunt. He never saw his parents again.

"Dr. Sonjee, I hope your injury is not serious."

"Peter, I have a mild concussion and an ankle sprain. I am just under observation. I may be discharged tomorrow."

"I am glad to hear that. Do you recall anything about why I came to you some twenty years back?"

I asked him to have a seat and pull up his chair close to me.

"Yes, you were involved in an automobile accident. I believe it was near the St. John's University campus, and that a fourteen year old boy had died."

Peter stood abruptly and went to the window. After a few minutes, he returned to his chair.

"Dr. Sonjee, perhaps when you've recovered completely from your injury, we can have dinner together. What caused your injuries? The news report gave no details."

"Peter, you may recall my office is located in Brooklyn Heights. Was it yesterday? I guess, it was. What day is today? After seeing my last patient, I went on a long walk on Henry Street, towards the Greenwood Cemetery. I was crossing a street near the entrance to the cemetery and I was just about three feet from the sidewalk when I was struck by a car. A split second before I was hit, a boy pulled me away. The car hit me lightly and the right front tire bruised my right ankle."

"Dr. Sonjee, who was that boy?"

"A crowd gathered. The driver, a woman, was hysterical. She kept saying, 'I didn't see him.' I was dazed. People said that the driver had made a left turn on the green light and didn't see me."

"Dr. Sonjee, did the witnesses say anything to the Police?"

"Yes, Peter, as of now, the Police haven't filed charges against the driver and according to witnesses, even the boy who pulled me out of harm's way, reported to the Police that I was in the wrong."

"Dr. Sonjee, do I understand that without the helping hand from the sidewalk you would be much worse off? "

I smiled and said, "As the Americans say, someone up above was watching over me, a right person at the right time and the right place. I could have been severely injured, disabled, or dead."

"Who was that young man?"

"David something. I asked him to give me his name and address so that I could thank him personally. As I was carried to the ambulance, he gave me a piece of paper and left. I still have that piece of paper."

"Dr. Sonjee, I might come along with you when you go to visit this boy. Incidentally, a new Jewish Deli has opened in Williamsburg. Let us have dinner there. I will call you in a couple of weeks."

It took me several weeks to improve sufficiently to return to work. I did not mind. I was able to read such books as 'History of British India' by Sir W. W.

Hunter, and 'Women of the Raj' by Margaret MacMillan, that lay unopened on my coffee table.

Peter called one evening. I had kept that piece of paper with the name and the address of the young man, but there was no phone number, nor was there a listing in the phone directory. Peter and I decided we would have lunch and walk over to the house given in the address. It was 667 Orange Street, an elegant residential area of Brooklyn.

After a leisurely lunch, we started walking. Peter talked about his childhood in Germany, his colorful home in a village not far from Frankfurt. His images of childhood were vivid, colorful, full of pathos and humor. He never mentioned his parents who died at Auschwitz. I noticed that he was getting agitated and complained of chest pains.

We sat down on a bench on the street. I assumed that the memories of parents had disturbed him.

"Dr. Sonjee, I am sorry. You remember I had an episode of depression some twenty years ago and I came to you for consultation."

"Yes, Peter. It was after an auto accident that you were involved in. I had referred you to a psychiatrist friend of mine. A fourteen year old boy had died. It was near the St. John's University campus."

"It was winter of 1972", said Peter. "It was still dark. I am a very cautious driver. On the way to work, there were a number of school bus stops. I was driving very slowly. There was a group of children waiting for the bus. Suddenly out of a cluster of dark figures, someone ran in front of the car and I felt the impact. I hit the brakes. I was panic stricken. The children were crying and screaming. I took out a flashlight and got out of the car. A boy lay on the street, unconscious with a deep wound on his scalp with blood gushing out to the pavement. I started screaming. Several men and women had come. I was stunned. I started praying an old German Jewish prayer, but couldn't even remember the words. An ambulance came, then the police."

"Peter, you need not go any further."

"Dr. Sonjee, I have to finish. I can't help it."

Peter went through all the details. The boy had died in the Brooklyn Hospital. After lengthy investigations by the police, Peter was found to be innocent and no charges were filed.

"Initially, I felt relieved that I was innocent, that it was an act of God. On a rational and intellectual level, I had committed no crime. But gradually, I fell into a depression over the incident. I couldn't concentrate. My appetite vanished. That was when I came to you for consultation."

"Peter, it is getting a bit late," I reminded him. We walked slowly towards 667 Orange Street. I had started a practice in Psychiatry in Brooklyn in the early 1960's. Then, it was mainly Jewish. I was struck by the fact that Brooklyn was now a different world,with such diversity: a microcosm of the world.

I rang the door bell. There were footsteps, and the door opened a crack. A man, balding, with a suspicious look on his face peered out. I quickly took out the piece of paper and showed it to him. He snatched it from me, looked at the paper, then us.

"Sir, David saved my life. I am here to thank him personally. I am Dr. Sonjee a local psychiatrist. This is my friend, Peter."

The man shouted, "Eva, come here. There are two 'nuts' with a piece of paper. The handwriting on it looks like David's."

I reassured him that I had come to thank David personally. In the meantime, his wife, Eva, had come to the door. She looked at the piece of paper and then at us. Finally, she asked me for my business card, which I gave her. Again, she looked me over. Then, she said, "Please come in." The man asked us to be seated. I surveyed the dimly lighted room, which had old but elegant furniture and piles of books everywhere.

"How did you get this piece of paper?" the man asked.

I recounted the story of the automobile accident. I described the boy, lanky, tall, crew cut, with a sweatshirt with 'Brooklyn Dodgers' on it. After I had finished my story, suddenly the man lunged towards me with hands outstretched. Peter was quick enough to come in between us. "Dr. Sonjee, you must have made some kind of a mistake. Let us leave." At this point, I heard Eva sobbing. The man sat down and said, "I am sorry, Dr. Sonjee." There was another long period of silence. I saw Peter at the edge of his chair. Eva stopped sobbing, left the room and returned with a faded photograph. She sat down and said, "Our son David died in an auto accident in 1972. He was waiting for a school bus. It was a dark early December morning. He darted across the street to meet his friends. There was a car going very slowly. Obviously, he assumed the driver would stop. He hit his head on the rear view mirror. The injury was massive. He succumbed. It happened near the St. John University campus. He was only 14. He would be 34 today. Now, you come with this piece of paper? It is his handwriting and his signature. We have lived in this home for more than thirty years. Dr. Sonjee, look at this photograph of our son."

She passed this photograph to me gingerly. It was the picture of the boy who had saved my life.

I mustered the courage to ask Eva the name of the driver of that car. She took some time, and with tears rolling down her cheeks, added, "Dr. Sonjee, it has been so long, but still so fresh. We have lived that scene in our thoughts, fantasies, dreams and nightmares."

I asked, "Madam, do you remember the name of the driver?" The man said, "His name was Peter Stein. You know, Dr. Sonjee, after twenty years, we still think, he could have honked or simply could have stopped. Yes, technically, he was innocent, but not in our eyes."

I looked at Peter and saw that he had slumped over. "Call 9-1-1 !" I screamed.

MY FRIEND'S NEW RELIGION

"You are planning to go to India on a leave to study religions?" I asked incredulously of my friend, Reverend Steven Phillips. "Yes, Dr. Sonjee, I have been thinking about it for some time, especially since I have known you."

We were having lunch at a restaurant in the French Quarter of New Orleans when the above exchange took place. I had started a private practice in psychiatry in the 1970's in this city on the Mississippi River because of its climate, culture, festivities, history and last but not least the Mardi Gras celebration.

I had known Reverend Phillips, an African-American Minister of a local Protestant Church, for about three years. A Lions Club in the parish of St. Bernard had once invited me to talk about Hinduism, and the Reverend was a member of this Club. At the conclusion of my talk, he came over to me and we became friends. We had been meeting twice a month for lunch every other Friday on a regular basis. I had found him quite knowledgeable about religions of the world. He had completed a Doctorate in a prestigious Theological Seminary in New York City. I listened to his analytical comments on various concepts and practices of all religions. My knowledge of religions of the world was very limited. In fact, Reverend Phillips knew more about Hinduism than I. There was one important difference: I was born and raised a Hindu and had experienced living Hinduism, with all its rituals and festivities.

My office was near Jackson Square and the Cathedral of St. Louis. I very much enjoyed the historic districts of this enchanting city.

"Reverend Phillips, why go to India? Why not Jerusalem, the holy place of three great religions of the world: Islam, Judaism and Christianity?"

"Dr. Sonjee, I am familiar with these religions but not so with Hinduism, Buddhism and Jainism. I want to be in India, to experience all the religions, including Islam. I wish to participate in the rituals, especially those of Hinduism. I will be gone for a year. The Bishop has already approved my Sabbatical. As you know, my wife has her own independent profession and we have no children. She is supportive of my mission."

"Reverend Phillips, do you realize how difficult your trip will be? India, from a distance, has a mystical charm, an abode of spirituality: I emphasize, at a distance. Yes, it is an enchanting land of huge contradictions, of an ancient civilization that is still living, but as you know, of unbelievable poverty, squalor, dirt and scenes that will shock you. Apart from that, you are Black. I am not sure that you will not experience discrimination on the basis of skin color. For you to go to India may be hazardous. Are you sure you are not going off the deep end?"

"Dr. Sonjee, I have studied India extensively. About my being black, I can always say that the great Lord Jagannath of Puri is referred to as 'Kalia, the Black One'."

At this, my friend gave a hearty laugh. Obviously, I was not able to dissuade him from this trip.

I asked, "Reverend Phillips, what is your mission? What will you be searching for in India? What will be the places you will visit? One year is a long time."

"Dr. Sonjee, you need not worry. I will be attached to the Church of India headquarters in New Delhi. The Bishop is arranging all the details. I will have an official of that Church accompany me in all the trips. Officially, I will be a Visiting Fellow at the Jawaharlal Nehru University of Delhi. I understand I will have access to all the libraries in the Delhi area. I will have staff to assist me in my research."

"Reverend Phillips, research into what? What are you trying to find out? There have been thousands of scholars over the millennia going into all these questions. I do not get it."

At this, Reverend Phillips became serious and for a moment had a faraway look. He responded, "Dr. Sonjee, I have been a minister for several years. I preach the message of love, of understanding and compassion for fellow human beings. Do you know how many times a year black churches are vandalized in Louisiana? I really do not wish to go into all that. You can look around yourself at the world scene. Religion is being abused as a divisive force. One of the Baptist ministers has referred to Hindu Gods as Devils. You look at the Middle East, Islam and Judaism being locked in a deadly conflict. You look at Northern Ireland. So, why am I going to India? I would like to find those common threads of all religions. And there is no better place than India."

I knew here was a determined and dedicated man of God who was turning to India in search of something abstract and undefinable, among the multi-religious and multicultural society of India. We continued our get-togethers. I prepared him for the trip, and answered his questions as best as I could. Reverend Phillips was going to visit various pilgrimage centers of Hinduism such as Varanasi, Mathura, Hardwar, Puri, Tirupathi, Dwaraka and also, Bodh Gaya, where Buddha meditated and attained wisdom.

Finally, the day came. His wife, Margaret and I saw him off in the New Orleans International Airport. Also, there were a number of people from his congregation.

"Dr. Sonjee, it is nice of you to come. I appreciate all the help in preparing me for this journey."

I responded, with a hearty laugh, "Journey in search of what? Truth, spiritual wisdom or the common threads of harmony among men? Or shall I say, a journey into the soul of man?"

We promised each other that we would keep in touch. I received letters from Reverend Phillips on a fairly regular basis. In addition, I was regularly invited to his church functions. Margaret was quite active in these functions and she too kept me informed of news from her husband. From all accounts, Reverend Phillips was doing well. Being under the patronage of the Church of India, he was invited to numerous Christian homes in Delhi. However, he did mention in one of his letters that invitations from Hindu or Muslim homes were few and far between. He was not sure if this was because he was black or Christian or both. There was no hint of bitterness in his letters. He gave good accounts of his visits to pilgrimage centers, but he hardly made any comments on his mission. He fell in love with India. He was immensely enjoying his visits and had plenty of time to interact with others. Both Margaret and I were relieved and happy that he was doing so well.

A year passed by and we were there to receive him at the New Orleans International Airport. It was a huge and warm welcome. I waited for my turn. He gave me a hug and said that we should resume our lunch program. He was radiant with joy and obviously happy to return home.

For several lunch sessions I listened to him about his experiences. He had maintained a daily diary of his contacts, activities and above all, insightful jottings of his inner thoughts and feelings, as related to his original mission.

"Dr. Phillips," I asked one day, " what about your search for harmony among human beings? What about some insight into inter-religious conflicts? What about fundamentalism? What about religion being abused as a discriminatory and divisive force? The bottom line is: Am I right in saying to you that because you are a Christian, you are not as good as a Hindu, and because I am a Hindu, to put it another way, do you have a right to say that I should be converted to Christianity? Does a Muslim have a right or duty to fight a Holy War against non-believers? Does the Jewish state of Israel have a right to treat Arabs as sub-humans or on the reverse, do the Arabs have a right to treat all Jews as sub-humans? I could go on and on."

Obviously, I was making an attempt to bring him out into the open about his so-called spiritual journey to India.

Reverend Phillips smiled sweetly and said, "Dr. Sonjee, I am still in the process of formulating a new religion for the world. It will take some time."

We continued to meet for lunch and I began to come to the conclusion that Reverend Phillips was yet another Christian missionary who had gone to India and failed in understanding the soul of India. However, I wondered about his remark on something like a new religion for the world. It sounded something like Martin Luther of the 16th century who, rebelled against the papacy. That particular phrase bothered me, "a new religion for the world". I was now more or less convinced that the Reverend Phillips had indeed gone off the deep end.

"Dr. Sonjee, you remember I mentioned something like my developing a new religion of the world. You might think I am a megalomaniac, or that I have developed grandiose delusions. Look, I will continue as a minister in my Church. My life will remain mostly the same, but I am developing a synthesis of all religions to guide human beings in the 21st century."

"Reverend Phillips, are you developing a super-religion? I am not sure what you have brought back from India. Human beings do not need a new religion. You know what Freud said about religions."

"Dr. Sonjee, have patience. The Kiwanis Club of St. Bernard Parish has invited me to speak to them next Tuesday. I would like you to come. That will be my first opportunity to share my thoughts about the new religion."

I walked back to my office and I thought, my friend might be out of touch. I felt a bit apprehensive but I do not know why.

I turned up at the Kiwanis Club meeting next Tuesday. I had no idea what the Reverend was going to talk about.

I have to say his speech was brilliant. He gave a succinct summary of all religions: Shinto, Zoroastrianism, Judaism, Christianity, Hinduism, Islam, Buddhism, Jainism, Sikhism, Taoism and Confucianism. Naturally he had to be brief, but he dealt with the goals and the paths of attainment of all these religions.

Then, he, in a brief summary, described his search of spirituality in India. He mentioned that he, in India, had visited all the holy and pilgrimage centers of all religions. Finally, he propounded his 'new religion of the world', and the basic tenets were as follows: seeing and feeling God in others, seeing yourself in others and others in yourself, living in harmony with others and nature, fighting the evil within and without, and above all, full and pure love towards others regardless of religion, nationality, color or creed. I noted that the Reverend never mentioned

Jesus Christ, Allah or the Hindu Gods or any other prophets. He mentioned that all religions were great but that there was a greater religion, according to his beliefs.

I continued to have lunch with him on a regular basis. I very much enjoyed listening to him and in a way, I considered him my Guru. Within a year or so, he had given talks at various places in Louisiana and nearby Texas. His thinking about a new religion became sharper in focus. In his sermons in his own Church, he referred less and less to the Bible and Jesus Christ. Some privately complained to him about this deviation and his referring to other religions in his sermons.

During one of our lunch engagements in the French Quarter, he seemed pensive and sad. He was not very talkative. I knew there was something wrong. However, I did not press him. He was not quite himself. Again, I waited until he was ready to share with me. It went on for sometime.

I had invited him for dinner at one of the finest Indian restaurants in New Orleans, the Delhi Curry House. We ordered wine before dinner. Still, he remained moody and not very forthcoming.

Unexpectedly, while sipping his glass of wine, Reverend Phillips expressed thus, "Dr. Sonjee, you might be wondering about this change in me. You remember after we met, I had told you about Black Churches being vandalized in Louisiana. My church, even located in a predominately Black neighborhood of New Orleans, has been vandalized thrice during the past few weeks. One graffiti especially concerned me and it read, 'Nigger Phillips, you have become a Hindu, a Buddhist or a Muslim. We will lynch you'. You know Dr. Sonjee, we the Black people of America, came from Africa against our will. You know about slavery. You know about racial discrimination on the basis of skin color. Can you imagine, as a psychiatrist, the depth of despair, anger and confusion when a trusting black child first feels the arrows of hatred, based simply on color of skin? Even in your country, India, while traveling around, I felt that subtle discrimination. I have remained a Christian Minister. I am only trying to raise the level of consciousness and understanding from a synthesis of all the religions of the world."

"Reverend Phillips, I am shocked. There are hate-mongers in your own congregation. How are you going to cope with all this hatred?"

He ordered another glass of wine and said, "I will stay on course. Regardless of dangers lurking ahead of me, I will continue to define the new religion that I am developing. I had forgotten to tell you that I had visited Fatehpur-Sikri near Agra. You know, that capital city was subsequently abandoned. In 1575 Akbar built a House of Worship. Let me add here, according to both Indians and foreigners, Akbar was the greatest of the Mogul Emperors of India. In this House of Worship, Catholic Fathers of Portuguese origin, Muslim Sufis and Hindu Pandits met with the Emperor himself and discussed religion. In 1582, the Emperor and the learned men of many religions formulated a divine way of life compounded of ideas of many religions. It is called something like Din-i-Ilahi."

"Reverend Phillips," I interjected, "I am concerned about your safety. The messenger has a message but the recipient is deaf. Perhaps the timing has not come yet. Perhaps you should keep a low profile."

Reverend Phillips got up, came around, hugged me, saying, "I will do the duty assigned to me by God. If I do not, it will be a living death for me."

We continued our lunch meetings. Reverend Phillips talked a lot about his experiences in India. He was a keen observer and I had repeatedly encouraged him to write a book on his India experiences.

It was a hot and humid day in July that I was due to meet Reverend Phillips for the usual lunch. Today, he was late. He had always been so punctual. I felt a bit uneasy. All of a sudden, Margaret appeared through the door. It seemed she was crying. She came over to me, hugged me and told me to come out. I knew the news would be bad. There was a bench outside the restaurant. I heard music. I saw a small group of men and women dancing to the calypso. Margaret held my hand and gave me the following story, in between her sobbings.

"Dr. Sonjee, Steve is in the hospital with burns. He is serious but not critical. According to his doctors, he will recover fully. He was working late in his church office. It must have been around eleven. He heard some unusual sounds such as cars coming to the back parking lot. He heard some other noises, such as a window being shattered. The church kitchen and dining room face the back parking lot. By the time he ran to the area, the kitchen was on fire. He tried to put out the fire. Within minutes the fire fighters were there. Luckily for him, he came out to the parking lot instead of trying more to put out the fire. Apparently, it took about twenty minutes for the fire brigade to put out the fire. He is fully conscious. It is arson. According to the Police, there was an anonymous call to the newspaper, claiming responsibility and vowing to destroy people like Reverend Phillips, who was called an 'anti-Christ'. Steve has already forgiven the arsonists. He remembered his lunch engagement with you and wanted me to come here."

Margaret started sobbing again. I hugged her. We went to the hospital. Reverend Phillips met me with a smile, as usual very friendly and warm. Just looking at this man of God, a black minister in America and a victim of an arsonist, I couldn't help being tearful. Reverend Phillips held my hands and said, "Dr. Sonjee, you will probably advise me to refrain from talking about a new world religion. If I do that, it will be a living death. Incidentally, Dr. Sonjee, just within this week, there are reports of Hindu-Muslim riots in Coimbatore in South India, with eight people dead. In the village of Lakshmanpur in northern India today, a gang of 300 armed men shot and stabbed their victims for two hours. All the 61 dead belonged to the lower caste of the Hindu society. According to Police the gunmen appeared to be members of a paramilitary group drawn from the region's higher-caste landlords."

I told him I read about it in today's newspaper, dated December 3, 1997. Then, I mumbled, "Reverend Phillips, what do you have in mind?"

There was a moment of silence. Reverend Phillips groaned with pain, looked at his wife first and then, at me and said, "India is calling me, Dr. Sonjee. I can feel it in my bones. I will not be able to resist it. I will not go there as a Christian missionary. I will not make any attempt to convert people to Christianity. I will repackage what I have learned in India and take it back to your people. Is it a new religion? I do not know. Yes, I will return."

Both Margaret and I were stunned and speechless. I put my hand over his forehead and told him, "Reverend Phillips, you are talking like Mahatma Gandhi and Martin Luther King Jr. and you know very well what happened to them."

He smiled and said, "I know very well what happened to them. If that will happen to me in India or America, so be it."

TANGO IN TORONTO

"D r. Sonjee, I am Dr. Verghese. You are not seriously injured. You are lucky, the bullet glanced through skin just over your left shoulder. There are no vascular or nerve injuries. There will be no functional limitations. I notice, you were born in India, and that you are a Hindu. I also note that you have a private practice in psychiatry in Oakland, California. You are here in Toronto to attend the annual meeting of the American Psychiatric Association. I am originally from Cochin in the state of Kerala in India."

I opened my eyes and made eye contact with this strikingly handsome doctor, probably in his late thirties. I knew that I was in the Emergency room of the Toronto General Hospital, but I was still in a daze. I remembered that earlier in the evening, I had been walking alone on Twenty-First Avenue to the Four Seasons Toronto Hotel, where I was staying. Earlier in the evening, I had attended a symposium on "Mental Disorders and Violence."

I responded in a weak voice, "I am glad to meet you Dr. Verghese. Do you have the details of what happened to me? My memory is blurred. I was walking along this street. It was dark but there were people around. I walked by a Pizza Restaurant. Just after, there was a dark alley to my right. Then, I saw some shadowy movements in the alley. I had no fear or suspicion. I suppose, I was engrossed in my fantasies. Then, I heard distinctly something like, 'Bash that Paki, Bash that Hindu'. From across the alley, I heard a shot, and then, felt a sharp stabbing pain on my left shoulder. The pain was so sharp and intense that I staggered and fell on the sidewalk. I felt warm blood. Perhaps, I was unconscious at the time."

Dr. Verghese responded, "You seem to recall virtually all the details except for what followed. According to police who interviewed witnesses, two men were walking just behind you, perhaps twenty feet. They heard a shot and saw you stagger and fall. They ran to assist you. At that moment, there appeared two white males, in neo-Nazi outfit. One of these youths was about to kick you with his boots, but that kick landed on one of the men who had come to assist you. There was a scuffle and these two young men were subdued by your helpers and others who rushed to the scene. They have been arrested."

"But Dr. Verghese, how do you know all these details and that these young men were neo-Nazis?"

"Dr. Sonjee, they have interviewed the criminals. They belong to a neo-Nazi gang of Toronto. They have been previously implicated in vandalizing South Asian businesses in Little India. You know, Little India along Gerrard street has a number of

Indian restaurants and businesses. They have regularly indulged in what is referred to as 'Paki bashing', that is, attacks on people of South Asian origins in Toronto."

I was getting angry. I had escaped death, but my anger had no limits. I could not console myself. I was attending a professional meeting of the American Psychiatric Association in 1977 and I had fallen victim to racial paranoia.

"Dr. Sonjee, you will be discharged from the hospital. It is about ten now. I will accompany you to the Four Seasons Hotel."

"That will be very nice of you, Dr. Verghese. I am quite capable of getting there in a taxi, but I am apprehensive. I will take you up on your offer. Who were the men who might have saved my life?"

"Dr. Sonjee, from the police I have their names and the hotel they are staying in. Mr. Kruger and Mr. Simpson visiting from Dayton, Ohio, are in the Hilton. They too are attending a conference in Toronto. You will be interested to know that they are African-American."

For a moment, this fact didn't quite register with me. Then, in a flash, I could visualize a confrontation between two African-Americans and two neo-Nazis in this beautiful city of Toronto.

Dr. Verghese continued, "Dr. Sonjee, these two gentlemen are teachers in the Dayton, Ohio school district, and they were attending a teachers' convention. It was reported by the Police and witnesses that the skin-heads, during the scuffle, used the most vile and unspeakable language."

It was time to leave the hospital. Dr. Verghese and I walked to his car. He insisted on accompanying me to the lobby of the hotel. He gave me his home address and phone number and said, "Call me if you need any help."

I had a restless night. My plans for attending the psychiatric meetings were shattered. Enjoyment of the City of Toronto as a tourist was also destroyed on that sidewalk. During the next day, I was interviewed extensively by R.C.M.P. detectives, who were very kind and considerate. At the conclusion of the depositions, I was warned by these officers that very definitely I would be subpoenaed for the upcoming trial of these assailants. I decided to return home.

I called a friend of mine, a psychiatrist in Oakland, California who also had come to attend the psychiatric convention. He came over right away. Despite my anger and inner turmoil, I tried to reassure him that I was not seriously injured. My friend was a volatile personality and it was difficult to calm him down. He insisted that he accompany me to the airport for my flight to San Francisco. During the taxi ride to the airport, he was constantly talking about how difficult it had been to achieve justice and equality in human history. He referred to mass eviction of the Jewish citizens from Spain in the early 16th century, systematic assaults on and plunder of the Native Americans in the New World, virtual annihilation of the aborigines in Australia, slavery in the Americas and the holocaust.

I made an attempt to add a hopeful note by stating that both Canada and India belonged to the British Commonwealth of Nations and both were vibrant democracies. We were approaching the Lester B. Pearson International Airport. He responded, "Perhaps, we will talk more about this later on. But Dr. Sonjee, do not forget the sign on the entrance to the English Club in Bombay of pre-independence India which read, 'Dogs and Indians not Allowed'."

I resumed my normal activities. I received a letter from Dr. Verghese inquiring as to how I was doing. He had talked with officials and organizations in the City of Toronto and the Province of Ontario, who were actively engaged in combating racial discrimination and abuses of human rights. According to Dr. Verghese, the Province of Ontario was very keen on combating racism and discrimination on the basis of religion and ethnicity. I knew that incidents continued to happen in all large and small North American cities.

Only after returning to Oakland and slowly getting over the hurt, pain and anger, I decided one evening to call both of the African-American teachers in Dayton, Ohio. "Mr. Kruger, this is Dr. Sonjee in Oakland. I am the man you helped in Toronto early last week."

"Yes, Dr. Sonjee, how are you doing?"

"I am doing fairly well. How about you?"

"Dr. Sonjee, my friend Jim Simpson and I were really enjoying our visit to Toronto until that incident. It was a shock."

"Mr. Kruger, you and your friend put yourselves on the line of fire to protect me and to subdue those neo-Nazis, altogether an act of extraordinary courage and compassion. You saved me from an undignified, execution-style death as a victim of neo-Nazism on a sidewalk in Toronto. I thank you and wish you the best."

"Don't mention it Doc. We happened to be at the right place at the right time. Take care."

"Yes, thank you again, Mr. Kruger".

Then I called Mr. Simpson. However, it was a different type of conversation. He was the one who took the brunt of the kick from the neo-Nazi boots and he had not yet returned to work.

"Mr. Simpson, this is Dr. Sonjee the victim in Toronto early last week. How are you doing?"

"Hey, Dr. Sonjee, I am glad you called. I was thinking about you. I am not badly hurt, but the trauma to my psyche is almost unbelievable. I am obsessed with that incident and that vile language of a racist punk directed against tax-paying, law-abiding citizens."

We talked some more. I thought Mr. Simpson was developing a post-traumatic stress disorder in as much as he indicated that he had insomnia, night-mares and much anxiety. I gently suggested to him that he might need professional help and he agreed to consider it. "Mr. Simpson, I really feel bad. I hope you will heal soon. Thank you from the bottom of my heart."

I was not looking forward to going to Toronto to testify in the upcoming trial of these two neo-Nazis. It was not the court appearance as such but just being in Toronto that made me anxious. I have been a workaholic in America. During periods of great personal stress and even despair, I continued to work fairly effectively and without getting into substance abuse or even clinical depression. However, that incident in downtown Toronto haunted me.

In late August 1977, I received a call from the Public Prosecutor's office in Toronto informing me that the trial was scheduled for mid-September and that I would be served a subpoena. I was expected to testify. I called up Dr. Verghese the same evening and he invited me to stay with his family. He also indicated that he had been in regular touch with the Public Prosecutor's office and that both Mr. Kruger and Mr. Simpson were coming to testify. He and his wife were to meet me at the Lester B. Pearson International Airport on arrival. I felt immensely relieved that I was staying in their home rather than a hotel in Toronto.

The day of the departure for Toronto came too quickly. I was met at the airport by not only Dr. and Mrs. Verghese but at least a dozen prominent members of the South Asian community of Toronto. I was not expecting this kind of a reception. Obviously, subsequent to that incident in May, there were a number of meetings of prominent South Asians among themselves and their meetings with human rights organizations in Toronto. On our way to the Verghese home, I was informed that the group in the airport included representatives from India, Bangladesh, Pakistan and Sri Lanka. For the next couple of days, I was further interviewed more by attorneys prosecuting the case on behalf of the Province of Ontario and the R.C.M.P. detectives. My story remained the same.

The trial itself lasted two days. Besides me, Mr. Kruger, Mr. Simpson and R.C.M.P. detectives, there were other witnesses, who were involved in subduing the assailants. The Public Defender argued for mercy. The defendants came from disturbed family backgrounds. Both were high school drop-outs. They had no family or community support. During my long career as a psychiatrist in America, I had seen literally hundreds of such youths. Many of them were mentally disturbed but here in this Court of Law, I was there as a victim and not as a psychiatrist. I made frequent eye contact with the defendants—blond, boyish looking, pathetic, flat and awkward. I wondered if the Hitler Youth in the waning days of World War II looked like these two young people. They were found guilty and the sentencing date was set for October by the Judge. I had heard that they would be sentenced to twenty years in prison on being found guilty of attempted murder. Justice had been done but my anger for being violated on that evening in Toronto had not really subsided.

Dr. and Mrs. Verghese had told me that there would be a get-together in their home of prominent members of the South Asian community of Toronto, some members of the Provincial Human Rights Commission and the Member of the Canadian Parliament representing Toronto. It was going to be a celebration of victory for justice. I insisted that both Mr. Kruger and Mr. Simpson be invited to this gathering.

It was a typical South Asian get-together; lots of food, talk about home countries, talking at the same time and children running around. There was going to be a formal meeting and according to the hosts, anyone could make brief remarks. During this gathering, I had visited with both Mr. Kruger and Mr. Simpson, who seemed to be enjoying themselves.

Finally, Dr. Verghese called for attention and announced that the meeting would start. Dr. Hussain, a Pakistani in origin and now a prominent orthopedist in Toronto, made the following remarks: "Ladies and Gentlemen, today is a small victory. We love Canada. However, our fight for equality and justice for all will continue. We have to be on the alert as members of the South Asian community. 'Paki bashing' must stop totally. We are relieved that Dr. Sonjee escaped major injury or death. If something like this could happen to him, it could happen to us, citizens of Toronto. I am thankful to Allah that his life was spared."

Mr. Joshi, originally from Allahabad in India, made the following remarks: "I would like to express our sincere thanks to Mr. Kruger and Mr. Simpson for saving Dr. Sonjee's life. That kick by the skin-head was not only meant to hurt Dr. Sonjee but the entire South Asian community of Toronto." At this point, every one stood up and gave a warm applause to Mr. Simpson.

Mr. Joshi was followed by one Miss Khalida who introduced herself as a senior in the University of Toronto. Her family had come from Bangladesh. She said, "I have had sleepless nights since the attack on Dr. Sonjee took place. There are many, many victims of this attack besides Dr. Sonjee. This is not an isolated incident. 'Paki bashing', harassment and racial slurs have been occurring for years. It has been happening in all major North American cities. You know about the 'dot busters' in Jersey City. We have to be alert and vigilant."

A few more made brief remarks on similar lines, on maintaining unity among South Asian community groups to fight against 'Paki bashing' through non-violent, legal and constitutional means.

Mrs. Verghese suggested that I speak for a few minutes. I was reluctant but as she was the gracious hostess, I couldn't refuse.

"Ladies and Gentlemen, I appreciate your coming here this afternoon. It is kind of you to give me the same support, you provided to one another. Yes, the South Asian community in Toronto and in fact, all of Canada and USA have made immense contributions in the fields of science, medicine, engineering and all other major professions. It has added to the cultural mosaic of North America. The South Asians should be proud of their achievements in Canada. Let us not forget that Canadians and Americans have provided us with the milieu and educational opportunities for such outstanding achievements. Also, let us not forget that as citizens of Canada or USA, we have to give something back. It must not be, 'all take and no give'. It is not enough for me to be just a doctor. I have to give something more to my community in Oakland, California. It is not enough for the South Asian community of Toronto to be concerned only with their rights and be involved in only their ethnic activities. It has to be more, much more."

At this point, I asked Mr. Kruger and Mr. Simpson to come forward and sit by me on the sofa. They were reluctant, but cooperative.

I resumed my speech, "You are rightly and understandably concerned with attacks on members of the South Asian community in Toronto. However, did these two gentlemen ever think of race when they came to my rescue? Some of you know the history of slavery in various countries of the Americas. How would you feel if a child of Indian, Bangladeshi, Sri Lankan or Pakistani origin were teased, taunted, shoved and kicked in the school playgrounds just because of his or her brown skin? You would feel enraged. Do you feel the same rage when an African-Canadian child is subjected to similar abuse? How would you feel if you were called a 'Nigger' and given dirty looks in Toronto? You must not forget that not too many years back, the English in India used to call us 'Niggers, Blackies or Coolies'. By a sweeping judgment based solely on skin color, they made themselves superior. Some of you may not know that on an entrance to an English club in pre-independence Bombay, it was prominently written, 'Dogs and Indians not Allowed'."

At this point, I suggested to Mrs. Verghese that there should be a break for a few minutes. During the break, we had samosas and tea. I noticed that many people had congregated around Mr. Kruger and Mr. Simpson and were animatedly talking to them.

The group reassembled. Again, I asked Mr. Kruger and Mr. Simpson to sit by me on the sofa. I put my arms around them and resumed, "These two men are my brothers." At that point, my voice rose sharply and I pointed an accusing finger at the group, and almost screamed, "Do not forget the experience in Uganda when Idi Amin kicked South Asians out. In that country, the South Asians remained an elite community, keeping the native Africans at arms' length. Right or wrong, they were considered foreigners and exploiters. There was a racial divide. That racial divide must be broken down in North America. If these two men are 'Niggers', I too am a 'Nigger'. As long as any citizen of Canada or America is considered inferior simply on the basis of skin color, then, our fight is not over. Let me give this message to the South Asian community of Toronto: open your hearts and doors to citizens of Toronto who are of African origin. Make a special effort to invite them to your functions. Let this process start now. They need us and we need them. You will find that people of African origin are no different from us and they are a wonderful people. We, South Asians, must not hide behind our professional and financial achievements in North America and stay away from such burning issues such as racism, domestic violence and religious bigotry. All our countries in South Asia are tainted with gross human rights violations—virtual elimination of Hindus and Sikhs in Pakistan, continuing discrimination against the lower castes and tribes in India, the ongoing flight of Hindu citizens from Bangladesh, the horrors of the ethnic war in Sri Lanka, the history of mass rape of women in Bangladesh and the genocide by the Pakistani Army just prior to independence of that country. We must not repeat those mistakes in our new homelands. We must go out and extend our friendship to all. Once you open the doors to your heart to an

African-Canadian, or a Native Canadian or anyone else, you will experience a kind of joy that you might not have experienced before."

There was silence after I concluded. There was no applause but there were many tearful eyes. Some-one started singing "We Shall Overcome ...." and the group joyfully started singing this bitter-sweet song, holding hands.

I returned to Oakland the next day. Within a matter of days, I joined the Oakland Chapter of the National Association for the Advancement of Colored People. The first meeting I attended was on an emergency basis. It was related to several incidents of racism against African-Americans but there were some white Americans present in the meeting. I was the only person of Asian origin. At least, it was a beginning, I consoled myself.

Not too many months after that, there appeared a story on the front page of the San Francisco newspaper that many Asian owned businesses were vandalized and graffittied with Hitler's Swastika signs. Here was a message, virtually the same message that befell me on a street in Toronto.

THE BOY GOD

We met for the monthly Gita discussion group in my suburban home in St. Louis. I had started a private practice in psychiatry in this colorful city on the west bank of the Mississippi River in the heartland of America. Our group consisted of a few Americans who had earlier visited India or were deeply interested in Hindu scriptures and philosophy. Discussion on the Gita, the Song of the Lord, the central piece of Hindu philosophy, was open and free.

On this evening however, I, as the coordinator of this group, digressed, "Before we start Gita discussion today, I would like to report to you something that has been disturbing me. I read a report in one of the Indo-American weeklies that a certain Pakistani scholar in a Pakistani-owned radio station in Houston had denigrated Lord Krishna."

Marilyn interrupted, "Dr. Sonjee, Lord Krishna of the Gita?"

"Yes, Lord Krishna of the Gita. Gita is only a small part of Krishna philosophy. The mythology surrounding Lord Krishna is enormous. What this Pakistani scholar did was to depict Krishna as a playboy and not as a good role model. Apart from this narrow and bigoted view, this Pakistani was bringing Muslim hatred towards Hindus even to America. The sublime teachings of the Gita in which Lord Krishna is the Great Teacher was ignored by this Pakistani scholar. Even Lord Krishna's activities as a boy has its own profound human insight. What concerns me is that Jihad, the Islamic belief of fight against the non-believers and infidels was being brought to North America by hate-mongers in the garb of scholars."

Beth, a computer instructor in a local college, said "I know Krishna philosophy. I have been to Mathura and Vrindaban. During my student days at the University of California at Berkeley, I visited the local Hare Krishna Temple fairly regularly. Yes, he is definitely out to hurt Hindu sentiments, but I defend his right to freedom of speech." Others joined in. It was refreshing to have a debate, a free exchange of ideas, insights, and perceptions.

I said, "Lord Jagannath of Puri, in Orissa, represents Lord Krishna. Also, the Jagannath culture and philosophy incorporate the highest ideals of Buddhism and Jainism."

It was December of 1983 that I paid a visit to India. My Thai International Flight No. 314 from Bangkok to Calcutta arrived in the afternoon and that same evening, I took a train to Bhubaneswar, the capital of Orissa, about thirty miles from Puri. I had always enjoyed visits to this temple city. Here was the great temple to Lord Shiva, Buddhist and

Jain caves and monuments, and some of the finest architectural gems, such as the Mukteswara, Brahmeswara and Raja Rani temples. To set foot on Bhubaneswar was to feel the sacredness and spiritualism that has pervaded this city from prehistoric times.

I got settled in the New Kenilworth Hotel and developed a daily schedule of visits to temples, ancient Buddhist, Jain caves, monuments and antiquities. I enjoyed these forays into the distant past of Orissa. I started my first day with an early morning visit to Lord Shiva's temple for worship. The scenes and sounds around the temple had not changed much since my first visit some forty years back. There were shops with flowers, coconuts, incense, garlands, oil lamps with wicks, sweets and vendors of all kinds of goods. I was literally mobbed by a few priests, one of whom won out to accompany me to the inner sanctum. The scene there was of confusion, people jostling against one another, priests chanting, worshippers offering coconuts, flowers and coins, lighting the earthen oil lamps and putting them down reverently to the phallic symbol of Lord Shiva I was assisted by the priest in the worship ritual, which I performed with reverence and prayer.

I returned to the hotel and had a message that a Mr. Das was coming to see me at around two in the afternoon. I had lunch and waited for the visitor, whoever he might be. It was not until three that there was knock on the door. I invited the stranger in and had him sit down. He was a small man, perhaps in his seventies. He smiled and said, "Dr. Sonjee, I am

Ramakanta Das. I am sorry to intrude upon your time and vacation. I had heard from your elder brother that you were in Bhubaneswar for a few days. He was my classmate in the Ravenshaw College at Cuttack."

I offered my greetings to him and waited. He asked a few questions about my life and work in America. He informed me that he was a retired professor of History. We had a conversation for almost an hour by now. I had mentioned that the Pakistani Muslim scholar in Texas ridiculed Lord Krishna. I told him about our Gita discussion group in St. Louis. I asked him, "What do you think of this Islamic scholar's remarks in Houston, Texas?"

He responded, "Dr. Sonjee, we Hindus are known as idol worshippers with all kinds of ceremonies, rituals, pilgrimages to our Holy sites such as Hardwar and Puri. However, underneath all this, there is a system of spiritual philosophy which is profound. In the very core of this philosophy, there is the deep faith, which has sustained us for millennia."

"Mr. Das, what is this faith? I am struggling with this myself. I was, as you know, raised in a very religious and spiritual Hindu Brahmin family, but having lived in America for so long, I have doubts about myself, as to whether I am a real Hindu or just a pretender without any real convictions."

"Dr. Sonjee, the fact that you are renewing your faith through your Gita discussion group in distant America speaks for itself. If you have time, I will relate to you some true stories, perhaps indicating how difficult it is to comprehend the concept of faith."

"Dr. Sonjee, this is a true story, I can assure you. It was the month of May in 1950 and the height of summer. I am sure you can remember how harsh the summer months are: a parched land, hot days, a brown and dry landscape, plants, trees, animals and human beings all drooping in fatigue. Life at times seemed to stand still. In those harsh days of summer, there were reports that a boy perhaps ten years old, was found under a tree in the typical Lord Krishna pose."

I interrupted, "Mr. Das, where was it and can you please describe that pose?"

"Dr. Sonjee, it was in a village near Talcher. That pose was feet crossed in a standing posture and a flute on the lips, as if playing a tune. This news spread like wild fire and that Balakrishna, that is, Lord Krishna as a Divine Boy had returned as a re-incarnation. Also, it was mentioned in the media that just viewing this boy caused miraculous cures. You can imagine the impact of this news in the villages and towns of Orissa, and even nearby states. People started coming in a trickle, then by the busload, by bullock carts, groups of people walking and then, trains to the nearest station arriving jammed with people."

"Was the government of Orissa prepared to meet this emergency?"

Mr. Das laughed and said, "We are talking about faith. We are talking about magnetic ties between a Hindu and God and with the added benefit of cure from an illness just by viewing the Boy God. Regarding your question, you have forgotten your country. What to speak of public health measures such as supplying clean drinking water and making sanitary arrangements, the Government started issuing one statement after another, warning people not to come but making no concrete arrangements for protecting them. Here was a demonstration of faith of the Hindu, but remember, faith also destroys. Utter destruction was let loose by a cholera epidemic. First, it was a few, the Government denying that it was cholera, but then, funeral pyres were lighting up within miles and miles of that village. There was chaos and panic. It was as though Yama, the God of Death, had taken over. Finally, the Government woke up and started bussing sick people to nearby hospitals and to the Medical College Hospital at Cuttack. But this so-called premier hospital didn't have enough beds, medications, supplies or personnel to deal with the massive emergency. Patients, critically ill, were placed outside under the open sky."

"Mr. Das, was there an estimate as to how many succumbed to cholera? Did the Government punish the people who neglected their official duties? Was anyone held accountable? Did the Government set up an enquiry commission to go into all aspects of this tragedy? Were there any recommendations to prevent such tragedies in the future?"

"As usual, the Minister of Health set up a Commission of Enquiry. It held hearings for a couple of years. By the time this Commission came out with recommendations, the tragedy had been forgotten or rationalized as Destiny, both by the people and the Government. Such reports gather dust in the corridors of power."

I sighed and said, "What a great tragedy. But Mr. Das, what happened to the Boy God Krishna?"

Mr. Das looked out of the window for a moment. "Dr. Sonjee, when cholera broke out, there was mass hysteria and panic and amidst the chaos and confusion, the Boy God Krishna disappeared. It remains a mystery even after thirty years."

"Mr. Das, could this kind of disaster happen again? Have the Government and people learned anything?"

"Dr. Sonjee, such disasters will not only continue to happen but have happened since then. Our blind faith in our Gods and Goddesses nurture us at times and kill us at other times."

It was evening. Mr. Das and I retired for dinner and then went on a stroll around the great Shiva Temple. One could feel the faith of the people.

I requested that Mr. Das come the next morning for another visit. He came at around eight. We decided to visit other antiquities around the Great Temple. It was a pleasure to listen to this man. He went back hundreds of years talking about this temple city. We returned for lunch and I asked Mr. Das if he had other stories on the faith of Hinduism.

"Dr. Sonjee, a few years back I was visiting with a highly educated person in the Jagannath Temple complex at Puri. He told me a story, which is unbelievable, but to him, it was true. He was a functionary of the temple administration for many, many years. He told me that he was returning home around midnight after completing his duties. It was the height of the monsoon season. It was a rain storm, thunder with lightning, and streets completely deserted. He was fearful that the lightning would strike him. He saw a figure coming from the opposite direction. He was fearful that it might be a ghost or a witch. The figure came closer and closer. He stood transfixed with the flash of a lightening, and was astonished to see a very beautiful woman. 'Who are you, going alone at night?' The figure stopped, 'I am Parvati, Lord Shiva's consort. I am returning home. We, Goddesses in the Jagannath Temple complex, had a late night meeting.' My friend said that she suddenly disappeared and immediately the rain storm subsided. He was convinced that his life had been saved through intervention of the Goddess."

I shook my head from side to side not knowing what to make of this story. After a moment of silence, I asked Mr. Das, "What do you think of it?" His response, "Faith of the Hindus." He resumed, "Have you seen the famous Nrusinghanath Temple near Padampur at the northwestern corner of Orissa?"

"Mr. Das, I have heard about the temple with the beautiful idol of Nrusinghanath, an incarnation of Vishnu, half-lion and half-man. I also know the story. But Mr. Das, you have some story about it, I assume."

"Yes, Dr. Sonjee, I have heard that the temple was built in the 15th century by one local King. The legend goes like this. A farmer was tilling his land one morning and his wife was assisting him in some other chores. When the land was ploughed on a certain spot, a liquid oozed out of the ground, which looked like blood. The farmer and his wife were in a state of panic and ran to inform the village elders about this extraordinary phenomenon. Elders and learned men from the village assembled on the spot. The fluid was still oozing. The village elders decided that it was blood and God was giving a message to the people and the King. Word was sent to the King and his ministers. It took a couple of days for a royal delegation to reach the spot. It was headed by the Chief Minister of the King. The delegation visited the spot. The sight was unbelievable, red liquid oozing out of the farm land. The Chief Minister decided, after listening to various opinions, that a temple to Nrusinghanath should be built on that exact spot."

"Mr. Das, is there any kind of documentary proof or records?"

"Dr. Sonjee, if and when you visit this temple, you might talk to villagers around the temple. Generally, they all subscribe to this legend, with minor variations. Remember, I told you, faith sustains us Hindus."

I invited Mr. Das to come visit with me the next day. I wanted him to relate more examples of faith, especially in regard to Jagannath worship.

Mr. Das came in the early morning. Again, we took a walk to the Temple of Lord Shiva. On this visit to Bhubaneswar, I was neither a tourist nor a devotee, per se, but mostly listening to this very learned and wise man, on the history of the temple city, giving glimpses of various dynasties that ruled Orissa and the Kings' obsession with temple building.

On returning to my room, Mr. Das resumed his stories, this time relating to Lord Jagannath.

"Dr. Sonjee, have you heard about the great Oriya

poet of early 16th century?" I pleaded ignorance. He continued, "I am sure that you know about Bhaagavata. Many Oriyas read it daily in their homes as part of the worship ritual."

"Yes, Mr. Das, my late grandmother used to read it daily for a few minutes. I only regret that I never asked her, as a child, to explain it to me."

"Dr. Sonjee, when you go to Puri, please visit the Satlahadi Matha, the Monastery of Seven Waves. It is located right on the sea near Swargadwar, the Gateway to Heaven cremation ground. It is associated with memory of Jagannath Das who had translated the Sanskrit Bhaagavata into Oriya. The story goes that, Jagannath Das, a great devotee of Lord Jagannath, asked the sea to recede by 'seven waves' so that he could find the ideal place to meditate and contemplate. I suppose, his contribution to Oriya culture and literature is associated with this belief and the monastery, still standing, is aptly named the 'Monastery of Seven Waves'."

I responded, "It is a fascinating story, a man meditating and contemplating on the beach at Puri and such activity being associated with the great Bhaagavata."

"Yes, Dr. Sonjee, in large villages in Orissa, there is a specially erected platform where this great devotional literature is read in front of the villagers. Dr. Sonjee, I am sure you are aware of the Hare Krishna movement in America and Europe. Their philosophy is Vishnu worship and Lord Jagannath is the manifestation of Vishnu. Actually, Sri Chaitanya popularized chanting and worship, which the Hare Krishna movement has adopted. So, we walk towards the Radhakanta Monastery, just a third of a mile from the main temple. Sri Chaitanya visited Puri in 1510 A. D. and made this monastery his center for religious mission and propagation of Vishnu culture. Some of his personal belongings are still preserved here. In this monastery, there is continuous chanting of the names of the Lord day and night."

"Mr. Das, what happened to Sri Chaitanya?"

"Dr. Sonjee, I am glad you asked the question. Some people believe that one day this great devotee of Lord Jagannath just disappeared." Mr. Das continued, "Of course, the ultimate experience of renewal of faith is to come to the Car Festival of Lord Jagannath. I understand this festival is now celebrated in several American cities such as New York, San Francisco, Nashville and Los Angeles."

I interjected, "But Mr. Das, what has faith to do with this great festival of the Lord of the Universe? I have attended this festival many years ago. Yes, for me, it was a grand spectacle, a celebration of the Lord's journey. I have to admit I didn't feel any particular upsurge of faith in my heart."

Mr. Das seemed lost for a moment and then, proceeded, "Dr. Sonjee, I am sure you know, that during the car festival some devout pilgrims would seek death under the chariot of the Lord of the world."

I interjected, "But that is all history now. After the British conquest of Orissa in 1803, the custom died down. By 1818, it was reported by a British officer that only three people had sought this kind of death or shall we say, suicide."

Mr. Das added, "You, as a psychiatrist, label it suicide. Could it be a matter of faith? Could it be that these pilgrims were seeking salvation? The story has come down in our family for generations that one of my forefathers sought salvation or freedom of the soul by sacrificing his life under the wheels of the chariot of the Lord of the Universe."

In our Gita discussions group after I returned from India, I related my encounter with Mr. Das at Bhubaneswar, the stories of Faith he related to me. Surprisingly, every member in our small group had a story of Faith. After hearing their stories I told them one about my family. According to anecdotal history, a great grandmother of my maternal grandfather had sought the supreme sacrifice, that is, placing herself on the funeral pyre of her deceased husband, with the name of God on her lips when the fire consumed her. It happened in 1835. For a moment, there was silence. Then Eileen, who has been to India many times, started softly chanting, "Hare Krishna, Hare Ram ......"

THE CABLEGRAM

D
r. Sonjee was having a particularly traumatic and stressful week. He was training to be a psychiatrist in a big University Medical Center in the Midwest. One of Dr. Sonjee's patients had accused him of not understanding American culture and thus implied that he couldn't really be an effective psychotherapist for her. Dr. Sonjee had come from India to this prestigious Medical Center in the heart-land of America. He worked very hard, sometimes driving himself. He was missing his country and at times wondered what exactly he was doing in America. In addition his friend and colleague, Dr. Nelson, was depressed after his patient committed suicide on the psychiatric unit. He had tried to comfort his friend but he was preoccupied with his own self-doubts. He looked outside his apartment and saw that it was stormy; snow was falling heavily, it was dark. He realized there was also a storm raging inside him. He looked down on the street below, and began to think about the warm and busy street in Calcutta. A blast of cold air on his face took away that fantasy.

The telephone rang. Dr. Sonjee was not too unhappy, expecting he was going to see a psychiatric emergency. He picked up the phone and the hospital operator said, "Dr. Sonjee, you have a Western Union cablegram from India. Please come and pick it up."

"I will be there soon," Dr. Sonjee replied. He dressed in haste, with much anxiety, and he could feel his heart beating against his chest wall. He hurried through the corridors of the vast hospital to the message desk and picked up the cablegram. He wanted to retreat to a dark corner to open the envelope. He looked at it to be doubly sure it was for him. His hands started trembling. He found a lone chair in an empty examination room and opened the envelope. He was so clumsy. He looked at the message. For a moment the paper looked blank, just dots and lines. Then, slowly, the words came into focus and it read, "Ram critically ill. Wants to see you." Dr Sonjee felt staggered, his mind a complete blank. He went to the rest room and washed his face with cold water. As he came out of the rest room he almost ran into Nurse Mary Jane. She immediately thought there was something wrong and said, "Dr Sonjee, can I help you?" He knew that she was a highly intuitive psychiatric nurse. He said quickly, "Thanks, Mary Jane, I will be fine." She left him alone.

Dr. Sonjee looked at the message again and again. Ram was his closest friend in school in India. He recalled that there was hardly a day that they were not together. They laughed and cried together, they played together. Dr. Sonjee recalled that he himself was considered a brilliant student, but that his friend

Ram was unmotivated and shy. He remembered how he would spend endless hours helping Ram in his studies. He remembered how his friend was a prankster, always making jokes. He was so fond of Ram. He recalled with a smile how Ram thought he had fallen in love with a girl with whom he had never spoken. He recalled in those days how boys and girls in school were not allowed to talk to each other. He remembered with much amusement the time he, Ram and other friends walked around the girl's house several times after school so that Ram could have a glimpse of her. He saw a thousand faces of his friend, Ram, mostly smiling, joking and talking. Then the message in the cablegram slowly displayed a face of Ram, in pain with a vacant look. He couldn't think. He slowly got up from the chair, started walking towards his apartment in the hospital complex. He looked over his shoulder suspiciously, wondering if Mary Jane was watching. Actually he thought it might be very worthwhile to have a talk with Mary Jane, but rejected it. He noticed that the storm was still raging outside. Upon reaching his apartment he didn't feel like undressing, and staggered into his bed.

It was bright sunshine when he woke up the next morning, after a restless night. He tried to think but his mind was a blank, then he slowly began to remember the cablegram from India. He searched for the cablegram without success. He began to feel better as he became convinced that it was just a bad dream.

He took a shower, got dressed, and thought he might call up his close friend, Marv, to go for breakfast at Tony's. He and Marv shared a fondness for Tony's because it was the most inexpensive, small restaurant in town. He didn't like to spend money, and neither did Marv. He called his friend who knew instinctively what he wanted. He simply said "See you at 8:15 at Tony's." As Dr. Sonjee was walking towards the restaurant he went over and over the nightmarish dream. He even wondered if the stress of being a psychiatrist in training was too much for him. He thought about his friend, Dr. Nelson, and the suicide. He knew that life was not pretty at times.

At Tony's the waitress greeted both of them with a cheery, "Good morning." Dr. Sonjee always admired the perpetually cheerful waitress. She knew what they wanted for breakfast, and left. Marv saw that his friend looked pale and anxious. He simply waited, being a man of much patience, warmth and understanding. Then Dr. Sonjee slowly began to relate to his friend his frightening dream about his friend in India, Ram. As he was going through the whole dream, he felt a piece of paper in his right coat pocket. His heart sank for a moment. He picked up the paper, wondering what it was, as he was not used to putting loose pieces of paper in his pockets. He opened it slowly and read the message from Western Union, "Ram critically ill. Wants to see you." The words in the message seemed to do a grotesque dance to his eyes. He slowly handed over the piece of paper to Marv.

The next day Dr. Sonjee made all the arrangements to fly to India. It was well over three days later that he arrived in his little town in the heart of India. He was met at the train station by his own brother, who took him straight to Ram's hospital bed. He walked up to Ram with folded hands and saw that his friend was surrounded by his wife and five children. He had not seen them in four years. He went to Ram, held his hands, clasping them, and tears began rolling down his face. Was there a faint smile on his friend's face or was he trying to tell one of his old jokes? He noticed that his friend looked like a skeleton, but the play of that mischievous smile seemed to persist until he lapsed into a coma. He knew in his heart that his friend had waited to say a final "Good-Bye" to him.

It was fully twenty-one years after his friend's demise that Dr. Sonjee again visited his small town in India. He had such a busy schedule. He could hardly recognize some streets. Sometimes he even wondered if he really grew up in that town.

Today was a nice day. He had such wonderful visits with his family members. He thought he deserved a brief nap. Soon he was fast asleep and it seemed like only a few minutes when he was interrupted by a persistent knock on the door. He put on his shirt and combed his hair. His niece, Savitri, opened the door and announced that a woman had come to see him.

Dr. Sonjee went to the front room and greeted a middle-aged female in a white sari. She folded her hands and said, "Dr. Sonjee, do you recognize me?" He seemed perplexed. After all he had not been in this town for a long twenty-one years. She looked straight at his face and said, "I am Ram's widow." He got up slowly from the chair and proceeded to hold her hands. There was a long silence and blurry eyes.

Dr. Sonjee knew they had much to talk about, remembering the last days of Ram and what they shared together the last hours in the hospital. He began telling her about the cablegram he received in America, his air dash to India, his night journey from Calcutta in a fast express train, and his visit with Ram and that enigmatic smile and subsequent lapse into coma. At that moment he saw that the widow was sobbing uncontrollably. Dr. Sonjee went up to her with folded hands, and waited.

The widow stopped sobbing but tears were rolling down her face as she said, "I wish you had come to say good-by to him. Before he lapsed into a coma he was in a delirium and he kept repeating only your name as if it were a mantra. When he had a lucid period on the morning of his death he asked me to send you a cablegram. He even told me what to say in the cablegram, 'Ram critically ill. Wants to see you.' I wrote it down on a piece of paper but it was too late to send a cablegram to America." Slowly she reached down her blouse to her bosom and pulled out the crumpled piece of paper and handed it over to Dr. Sonjee. She added, "He passed away the same day with a peculiar smile on his face. I knew you would come someday to say goodbye to him."

Dr. Sonjee recalled the cold and snowy night in America twenty- one years back. He and the widow slowly walked to the window and looked at the sky, bright and beautiful. He spotted a white cloud in the sky and there he could see his friend's face with that enigmatic smile.

THE FREEDOM FIGHTER

My friend John was an incurable India lover. He was born in a small town in Kansas, finished high school there and did his undergraduate studies at the University of Puget Sound in Tacoma. He received his Masters of Library Sciences from the Berkeley campus of the University of California. In the early 1970's, while he was still an undergraduate student, he toured India, Sri Lanka, Thailand and Nepal studying Religions of the World.

John and I met in the late 1970's. I had started my private practice in Psychiatry in San Francisco and John was a teacher of Library Sciences at the University of California. During the late 1970's and early 1980's, the number of people immigrating from India rose rapidly in the greater San Francisco area. With the new people came a marked increase in Indian cultural activities. Despite being a busy psychiatrist in this community, I made it a point to attend as many cultural activities as I could. Each time I went I noticed a young white male, thin, with a beard, intensely expressive. He would come alone and have no conversation with anyone. One day during the intermission of a classical dance function I approached him and introduced myself.

"Would you like to have a cup of coffee with me after the function?" I said. "I am Dr. Sonjee. He responded with a big smile and said in broken Hindi, "Ap Indiase Ayahen?" meaning, "Are you from India?" I told him that I was originally from the State of Orissa, famous for Odissi classical dances.

After the show we had coffee and I was hardly aware of how much time had passed. I found John very knowledgeable about Indian history and Hindu philosophy. We became good friends and enjoyed getting together once a week to visit and have lunch. I always looked forward to our meetings. He talked about anything related to India. I admired his insight into the dynamics of India's history and culture. Even though I was from India, I found him quite analytical and objective about my country. I shared with him my personal upbringing in great details, the colorful Hindu festivals of Orissa, including the Car Festival of Puri, and our rituals and practices. It was during one of our get-togethers in 1983 that I told him I had decided to take a brief trip to India. He was happy for me and asked about my itinerary. It was perhaps about a month later when John said, "How would it be if I come along with you? Since you are mostly going to Orissa I'd like to pay a visit to the land of my previous birth, especially in the company of a devotee of Lord Jagannath."

I was a bit surprised by this proposal. I knew John must have thought very seriously about it.

"Yes, John," I told him, "I do visit the Jagannath Temple and the Lingaraj at Bhubaneswar, just as my forefathers have for centuries. However I am not a tourist in Orissa. I go for family visits and to re-live the experiences of my childhood. You are a scholar and since this would be your second visit to India you probably would like to see the Taj, visit Delhi and Varanasi and the wonderful tourist places in Rajasthan. Even though you would not be allowed to visit the inner sanctum of Lord Jagannath, you could visit Puri and Konarak."

I felt bad that I was rejecting his offer, but I felt it would be quite awkward to have this American fellow come along with me wherever I went. He obviously sensed my discomfort as he smiled and said, "Dr. Sonjee, I will not be going as a tourist. I wish to come with you as a brother. I am sure you understand the depth of what I am saying." I could not turn him down. So we continued our weekly lunch meetings, planning our trip to India, and in December we were on our way.

John was a very good companion. We arrived in Calcutta where we spent two days touring such places as the Victoria Memorial, Fort Williams, and Job Charnock's Mausoleum in the courtyard of the St. John's Church. John was very knowledgeable about Calcutta and Bengal history. He told me that Job Charnock was an English adventurer and employee of the East India Company and founded Calcutta in 1690 during the reign of Aruangzeb. We also visited the ancestral home of Subhas Bose who had escaped from Calcutta to Germany and Japan during World War II, and led the Indian National

Army from Singapore and Burma. We visited the Kali Temple, Ochterlony Monument, the Writers Building and the Asia Society Building.

John and I took a walk around the Raj Bhavan, now the residence of the Governor of West Bengal, once the seat of British power in India, and the former home of the Governor General of India before the capital was shifted to New Delhi.

John made the remark, "You see, Dr. Sonjee, this imposing building was modeled after the Kedleston Hall of England and completed between 1799 and 1805. "

"Expansion of British imperial hold on India started from this building," I added, "Even the conquest of Orissa in 1803 was plotted from here."

We took an express train to Sambalpur where we visited my relatives and friends. There was a curiosity about him from all quarters and personal questions directed to him, which John handled with humility, charm and humor. During our stay we visited the Samaleswari and Pataneswari Temples. John was allowed into the inner sanctum of the Samaleswari Temple and to participate along with me in the prayer ritual. "Samaleswari is the presiding deity of Sambalpur," I said to John. "This temple goes back to about 1575 when Akbar was the Moghul Emperor at Agra and the Kingdom of Sambalpur had just begun. This kingdom was taken over by the British in 1849."

"In one of our get-togethers in San Francisco," John said, "you mentioned a freedom fighter, Veer Surendra Sai, who fought a guerilla warfare more than a century ago. Can we visit his village?"

"You mean Khinda," I responded. "In those days Khinda was surrounded with thick forests, meadows with tall sal trees, close to the Ib River and the Maula-Bhanja hills. The forests were full of wildlife. It was almost an ideal location for guerilla warfare. Yes, we will visit Khinda on our return trip from the costal areas of Orissa." Obviously John's vast knowledge of India included early freedom movements.

While in the Sambalpur area John and I were invited to various family rituals, including a marriage function. His curiosity, charm, humor and understanding of Hindu culture made him immensely popular. His laughter was wonderful and infectious, and despite the language barrier he got along well.

One beautiful morning at breakfast I told John I was going to make a trip by myself to the cremation ground on the bank of the Mahanadi where my parents and grand-mother were cremated many years ago. He understood and stayed behind. He had no comments or questions. I had made this trip often during all my previous visits to Sambalpur. I walked to the bank of the river, which was an old river and not as beautiful as it was in my childhood. I imagined the spots were the cremations might have taken place. I became sad as I thought of my father's cremation, a ceremony I could not attend as I was sailing for London, somewhere on the Arabian Sea. I made a silent prayer.

Several weeks later, we left for Cuttack. "Cuttack is almost a thousand years old," I told John, "a city founded by the ancient kings of Orissa and subsequently under the Moghuls, the Marhattas and then the British."

John added, "Ralph Cartwright was the first British officer to visit Cuttack in 1633. He had an audience with the Moghul Governor, Agha Muhammad Zaman, a Persian born in Teharan and a prominent soldier and administrator."

I was very impressed with John's knowledge of the history of Orissa. John and I visited the ruins of the Barabati Fort, the Cuttack Chandi Temple and the Kadam Rasool, sacred place for both Muslims and Hindus. We visited my old college, the Ravenshaw, where I had been expelled by the British administration for participation in the Quit India movement of Mahatma Gandhi in 1942. We went to the second floor balcony of the West Hostel, facing towards the East Hostel. I pointed out to John the area where we would gather for hours and call upon the British Government to "Quit India" and "Victory to Mahatma Gandhi." I began shouting the same slogans as I remembered the events of 42 years ago. To my surprise John joined in.

John asked, "Dr. Sonjee, why were you suspended from college? You were just a freshman, certainly not a leader." I smiled and said, "It is still a mystery to me. I found out later that I was on a list of about fifty students who were identified as agitators by British Government detectives. Perhaps the only reason was that I was newly elected as Joint General Secretary of the Hostel, a student organization for cultural and literary functions of the hostel. Subsequently, however, I was allowed to return to the college."

"So you are a freedom fighter?" John quipped.

"Not exactly," I said, "except that my name went

into the official British records as an agitator of the Quit India movement. Would you like to meet a real freedom fighter, a man who spent years in British jails and was the leader of Mahatma Gandhi's Party, the Congress, in Orissa? I understand he is staying with his eldest daughter and her family in Bhubaneswar. He was several years older than I was, but I had heard about his student days at Ravenshaw College. His name is Mr. Jena, and he was originally from Puri. I'm sure you will enjoy listening to him."

Of course John was enthusiastic about his upcoming meeting. He had read extensively on Mahatma Gandhi and the freedom movement of India.

It was mid-January when we arrived at Bhubaneswar, where we stayed in the New Kenilworth Hotel at Gautam Nagar. We made inquiries about Mr. Jena's whereabouts and was told that he was residing at Satya Nagar. Before we visited him we decided to visit Konarak, Puri and around Bhubaneswar, the Dhauli, Khandagiri and Udayagiri complexes and the superb Mukteshwar and Raja Rani temples. I went to the Lingaraj Temple to worship while John, a non-Hindu, was not allowed to enter the temple complex.

One evening we just walked to Satya Nagar to the given address and knocked on the door. A young man opened the door and upon seeing us immediately went away and returned with another young man. I introduced us, "I am Dr. Sonjee. I am originally from Sambalpur and have been in America for many years. I am a Psychiatrist in the city of San Francisco. This is my friend John, who teaches library sciences at the University of California at

Berkeley. We are on a visit to Orissa. We would like to visit with Mr. Jena." At this both young men smiled and directed us to come into their living room and asked us to be seated. They both went in the other room and within a few minutes brought us a plateful of sweets and snacks and cups of tea. We sat in silence until a frail elderly man with a shawl wrapped around him walked in on the arm of a young woman. He seemed to be in pain but upon seeing us managed a faint smile. With assistance from the young woman he sat in a chair.

One of the young men stated, " Grandfather is ill. He had a stroke several years ago. Sometimes his mind is very clear and at other times he is quite confused. He can recall his early days clearly but not recent happenings."

I gently inquired of Mr. Jena, with folded hands, as to how he was feeling. In a very frail voice he responded, "Today I feel fair. Tell me about your American friend."

"Mr. Jena, this is John. He is a very close friend of mine. He teaches library sciences at the University of California. He is a student of the culture and history of India. He has a particular interest in the freedom movement of Mahatma Gandhi that led to the end of the British rule in India." At this point I couldn't help laughing and added, "John believes that one of his previous births was in India." At this there was laughter all around.

Then John asked Mr. Jena, "Sir, I would like to hear from you directly about your own personal experiences and participation in the freedom movement."

Mr. Jena seemed to come to life. He asked John to come and sit on a chair near him. He put his arm around him and said, "The Mahatma is dead in India, but perhaps alive in America. Yes, India is independent of the British but where is the economic freedom, where is the morality in Government that Gandhiji fought for?"

I gently interrupted, "Mr. Jena, my friend here would like to hear from you about your own participation in the movement." Mr. Jena said, "I am disappointed with what is happening in India now. Yes I understand your friend's interest. It is a long story. Do you have time? It might take days because what I am going to tell you will come from my heart."

"We will be in Bhubaneswar for a few more days," I said. "Yes we have time." John nodded in agreement.

Mr. Jena resumed, "You see I was born in 1908 into a poor family in Puri. My father was a poorly paid school teacher. It was 1919 when the Jaliana Bagh episode happened in Punjab. I was eleven then. Until then I had no idea that it was not normal for India to be under the British. After all, the British had been in Puri for more than a century and what was wrong with it? Somehow we heard about the firing on innocent citizens by the British forces in Punjab. Of course we had heard adults talking about Mahatma Gandhi coming from South Africa and leading the Congress. You see in those days there was a cloud of fear overhanging India. I felt the stirrings in my heart, the impact of this movement. While a student in the high school at Puri I kept myself informed about the Mahatma's movement, although as students we were keenly aware that any direct participation in street agitations or non- cooperation would result in suspension from school."

John asked, "Did your school go on strike at any time?"

"Yes", Mr. Jena responded. "Perhaps it was around 1924 that the Mahatma was jailed and we organized a strike in the school and a procession. When I entered Ravenshaw College in 1926 and during my four years there I was very active in politics. In 1929 Jawaharlal, as President of the Congress, gave the clarion call for independence and I decided right then that after college I would be a Congress worker and join the movement actively. I was first jailed in 1931. This followed agitations all over Orissa after the arrest of Gandhiji at the end of his historic Salt March. You might have passed by the Cuttack Jail. I was there for several months."

John asked, "How did you get along in jail?" Mr. Jena continued, "I was a political prisoner. We were treated fairly. I had no hatred towards the British. It gave me time to reflect. It gave me time to read and study the history of India and especially that of Orissa. I remember after I came out of the jail I was more determined than ever to actively support Mahatmaji. We organized the party in villages. Dr. Sonjee, I was very active in organizing the Congress Party in your Sambalpur area. You may not know that Gandhiji visited Sambalpur in 1934. I accompanied the Mahatma on that tour."

"I remember," I said. "I was only nine when Gandhiji visited Sambalpur. I saw him and that scene is deeply engraved not only in my memory but in my heart. Even now I remember exactly the spot on which I stood and the Mahatma walked by just three feet from me."

Mr. Jena continued, "When Gandhiji walked, he walked like Jesus Christ. Let me return to my role. It was in 1942 when the Mahatma called upon the British to 'Quit India'. After the arrest of Gandhiji and top leaders, India was in flames. Parts of Orissa were inaccessible to British forces. There were wide-spread arrests in Orissa on August 8. I was in Balasore on that day and immediately went into hiding. I managed to take a train to Calcutta, where I stayed for several months with friends. I was very active in the underground that used sabotage and guerrilla tactics, not guns, while keeping up the Quit India movement and our morale. After many months I decided to return to Orissa to continue the agitation. That was a mistake. I arrived at Cuttack Railway station one early morning and the Police were waiting for me."

"How did they know?" John asked. "I don't know," Mr. Jena said. "The British Government Police detectives must have infiltrated our underground organization in Calcutta. I was taken straight to the Cuttack Jail and I was not released until 1945."

We had a second visit with Mr. Jena. It was obvious John was moved with the personal accounts as described by Mr. Jena. It was like listening to one of the Mahatma's disciples. We attempted our third visit on January 23rd. Mr. Jena's grandson appeared at the door and told us, "Grandfather is not feeling well. The doctor said he probably suffered from a mild heart attack, but nothing serious. He advised total bed rest. Grandfather should feel better tomorrow, please come back then. Do not come on January 26, however, as that is the day of the Governor's Annual Garden Party, which is part of the Republic Day celebration, and we are expecting an invitation any day now."

We returned on the 24th and the 25th but were told on both days that Mr. Jena was not feeling well and seemed depressed. I asked his grandson if the invitation had arrived from the Governor's office. "Not yet", he said. "Maybe this evening."

John and I had a quick consultation and decided to go to the Governor's Office to check on the status of the invitation.

After much difficulty and persuasive language by both of us, we were allowed to meet a junior officer who was in charge of mailing out the invitations for the Republic Day party. Mr. Roy was very nice and said, "The invitations were mailed out more than a week ago." John said, "Please check the guest list to see if Mr. Jena is included. He is a well known freedom fighter. He has been invited to these parties every year." Mr. Roy went through the list several times said, "I'm sorry, Mr. Jena's name is not on the list."

We were in shock. We couldn't believe that he had been overlooked. Mr. Roy expressed profound regrets and added, "There were new invitees added this year and some people were dropped. I guess there has been pressure to include a number of young politicians, although I'm not sure who is responsible for the final list. I am very sorry."

We were ready to depart in great sorrow. Then John turned around and asked Mr. Roy, "May I please have a sample of the invitation card as a memento?" For a minute Mr. Roy appeared suspicious but then he smiled, "Sure. Please have one and show it to your friends in America."

It was late in the afternoon. We hailed a taxi and I asked John, "May I have a look at the invitation card?" John handed it over to me. The card was embossed in gold lettering. I told John, "It is a nice memento from the Governor's office of Orissa to take back to America." I saw John was a bit agitated and he abruptly told me to convey to the taxi driver to hurry to Mr. Jena's house. Only then was it clear to me that John was going to deliver the much anticipated invitation to Mr. Jena.

We arrived at Mr. Jena's residence around five o'clock. His grandson again answered the door and sorrow was written on his face. John insisted that we be allowed to see Mr. Jena. We walked up to his room and saw that he was gravely ill. We were told that Mr. Jena had suffered another heart attack and was in and out of consciousness. We sat down on chairs near his bed. John clasped Mr. Jena's right hand and at that moment Mr. Jena opened his eyes and smiled. John took the invitation out of his pocket and tenderly told Mr. Jena, "Here is the invitation to the Governor's Republic Day party," as he placed it in Mr. Jena's hand. I cannot forget that beautiful smile like a rose opening up in the early morning sun, and then Mr. Jena lapsed into a coma from which he never recovered. He passed away in the early hours of the Republic Day, January 26, 1984.

THE MAN WHO SOUGHT NIRVANA

I t had been almost half a century since I attended the great Car Festival of Lord Jagannath at Puri, in the Indian State of Orissa. Was it 1947 or 1948? I was not sure. My recall of it is spotty. I was not even sure if I had gone there as a devout pilgrim or as a tourist on a sightseeing jaunt.

Now I was looking forward to attending the same festival in America, in Golden Gate Park, San Francisco. I had been in private practice of psychiatry in San Francisco for a number of years. My office at Arguello Boulevard was just walking distance from the Park and I was keenly waiting for June 23, the date of the festival.

Sunday, June 23 was a cloudy day in San Francisco. I got up early and read several pages of the Bhagavad Gita, the centerpiece of Hindu philosophy. After all, Jagannath does represent Lord Krishna of the Gita. On my way to the park, I had breakfast in one of my favorite Chinese restaurants, the Bamboo Curtain. I saw many people of Indian origin, walking towards the Park. I was looking forward to a day of festivity, rituals and Mela, that ancient custom of getting together in the great Hindu festivals of India. I was walking along at a leisurely pace when I heard someone behind me, following me closely, "Dr. Sonjee, please wait for a minute. I hope you do not mind my coming with you to the Festival."

I stopped and greeted this white male with a "Good Morning". I looked at him closely and said, "But I do not think that I know you."

"Dr. Sonjee, I wouldn't expect you to. Maybe, it was three years back that I met you briefly at the Asian Art Museum of the Golden Gate Park. There was some sort of special exhibition of the miniature paintings of the Moghul Empire of India."

I laughed and said, "Lately my memory is not very good and I am sorry, I cannot recall the meeting you are referring to." I was about to continue towards the festival when he said, "I am George Hexton and I would very much like to accompany you."

George turned out to be a very pleasant and friendly companion. He was quite knowledgeable about India and all about the great Hindu festivals. I assumed he belonged to the Hare Krishna movement, but he was not in the Hare Krishna garb.

Both of us enjoyed the Car Festival very much, with the chariot of the Lord being pulled by devotees. It was a miniature version of the Great Festival at Puri; nevertheless, it had a certain spiritual significance for me. George seemed to participate well in this unique spiritual experience.

On conclusion of the program, I was ready to walk back to my office and I said, "George, I really enjoyed your company. Maybe, we will meet again. May the Lord Jagannath be with you."

"Dr. Sonjee, it is almost time for dinner. I am going to the China Moon Restaurant. Would you like to join me?"

During dinner we chatted mostly about Hinduism and the festival. At one point, George said, "Dr. Sonjee, you are a psychiatrist. You have studied Carl Jung's Theory of the Collective Unconscious."

I was not about to get into any discussion with George on this subject but before I could cut him off, he proceeded to tell me that he was haunted by recollections of his previous birth in India. My immediate reaction was that here was another offbeat American, who had some fascination for Hindu philosophy.

George must have sensed this and said, "Dr. Sonjee, have you visited the cremation sites on the River Ganges at Varanasi?"

"George, yes, I have been there twice, but why?"

"I can recall that I was cremated there in my previous life."

I started laughing and said, "George, do you expect me to buy your incredulous story?   First, the concept of reincarnation is a matter of faith for the Hindus, with profound philosophical significance; second, the Jungian concept of Collective Unconscious has been debunked; and third, even I as a Hindu, have much difficulty with this concept."

George was persistent that I hear out his story. I said, "George, if you insist, I will listen."

We made a date a few days later to meet for dinner at the Empress of China Restaurant in

Chinatown. George was very warm and friendly during dinner. He gave the following story, "Dr. Sonjee, do you recall that you told me on our first visit that you were from the state of Orissa? I was born in 1880 in your ancient city of Cuttack. Mind you, I have never been to India, that is, since my present birth."

"How do I know that you have not concocted the whole thing?" I responded.

"Let me finish. Dr. Sonjee, you might be familiar with that city. I was born in a locality called Maria Bazar. My father was a shopkeeper—general goods, spices, oil, rice, sugar, etc. I had a brother four years younger than me. My mother was illiterate, but a very devout Hindu lady."

I was getting impatient with this story, and just to test him, asked if he could recall his name in this so called previous birth.

"Yes, Dr. Sonjee, my name was Nilamani Sahu." I knew it was a typical Oriya name but still I suspected George was a master storyteller. I remained incredulous. He continued, "In those days, Cuttack was sparsely populated, full of trees. I went to school until the third grade. Around age ten, I started helping my father in his shop."

I gently reminded George that it was getting late, and I had a very busy schedule with my patients the next day, "George, let us come to Varanasi, cremation site of your previous birth."

"I had a relatively stable life at Cuttack. As a young man, I took over my father's business, got married, and became relatively prosperous. I was a regular devotee of Cuttack Chandi. I made annual trips to the Car Festival of Lord Jagannath at Puri."

I interrupted him, "George, anyone can read about this and make a story out of it."

"Dr. Sonjee, let me finish. With prosperity came greed. I became obsessed with money. It became my God, though I pretended that I was a great devotee of Jagannath. I went into the money-lending business and charged exorbitant interest. I hired local anti-socials to threaten the debtors. Apart from amassing money, I enjoyed the power over these people. On the surface, I pretended that I was a devout Hindu. The rituals and festivals in my house in Maria Bazar were celebrated with pomp. I would go around with folded hands to greet the guests. I would frequently utter the various names of Vishnu. When guests would complement me, I would give all the credit to Lord Jagannath."

"George, do you mean to say that you were leading a double life?"

"Not necessarily, Dr. Sonjee, I had convinced myself that I was a great devotee of Jagannath, Lord Shiva and the Goddess of Cuttack. Moneymaking was just a part of life. Yes, I was aware on a certain level of my greed and exploitation of people, but I believed that all my sins were washed away daily through my devotion and visits to temples."

"Do you recall any feelings of guilt? Were you ashamed of yourself? It appears that you harassed, exploited and threatened many, many families. Did you get any feedback from others?"

"Dr. Sonjee, of course, I was aware that people might be talking behind my back. In fact, I actively cultivated shamelessness because only then could I do anything that I wished."

"George, so far it is not much of a story. The world is full of such people. In summary, you were a shameless, sadistic, selfish, rich man, but more dangerous, because on the surface, you had all the pretensions of deep spirituality, and devotion to Lord Jagannath and Shiva and the Goddess Cuttack Chandi."

"Dr. Sonjee, you are getting impatient. There is no summary or finality to such stories. In any event, let me come to the incident that turned my life around. I distinctly remember that evening. It was the month of October, very pleasant. I went to the temple of Cuttack Chandi to pray and participate in the ceremonial ritual. I was returning home. On the way back, I had to pass through a mango grove near a pond. It was a bit late. I had walked alone on that path many times before. I heard footsteps behind me. I thought perhaps other devotees were returning home from the temple. I looked behind and could see only a shadowy figure. After I entered the mango grove, I thought that shadowy figure was just behind me and I heard this voice, 'Sir, the Goddess has directed me to kill you tonight. She symbolizes the triumph of good over evil.' I started trembling in apprehension. I protested, saying that I was a staunch devotee of the Goddess. He said something like, 'Your lackeys have been threatening to kidnap my only child, aged ten, and to kill him if I do not soon pay you back the money I owe you. My child, wife and I are living a nightmare day and night. I too went to the Goddess this evening for guidance and she gave me the order.' "

"George, did he have any weapon in his hand?"

"Dr. Sonjee, I could vaguely make out an axe raised over his right shoulder. I prostrated myself on the ground, touched his feet crying, asking him to spare my life and promised him huge sums of money. Then, I felt the axe strike my left shoulder."

"George, I am sorry to interrupt you. Am I to believe that you remember all these details from your previous life?"

"Dr. Sonjee, let me finish. I woke up in the hospital next day. You remember the huge hospital campus near Manglabagh of Cuttack. Luckily for me, the axe had missed my neck. That was in 1930. On recovery, I transferred all my business to my sons. I became a recluse. I gave up going to temples. I had a dream one night that I should go to Varanasi and wait there for Death, to attain Nirvana. My wife accompanied me to Varanasi."

"George, is it the end of your story? You died on the bank of our sacred River Ganges and were cremated. Thus you attained salvation. But it seems you did not attain Nirvana, that is, the end of the birth and rebirth cycle and the merging with the Brahman."

"Dr. Sonjee, it seems that way." He smiled and gave me his phone number.

In due time, this encounter with George had somewhat faded from my memory until I had a business lunch with a psychiatrist colleague in the China Moon. I called George the same evening. A female voice answered the phone. I introduced myself and told her about my encounter with George. There was a moment of silence. Finally, she said, "Dr.

Sonjee, I am Jane. George is my boyfriend. He left for India about three months ago for the Holy Hindu City of Varanasi. Just prior to his departure, he seemed obsessed with the idea that he had to go there to be an ascetic and die there to attain Nirvana. Dr. Sonjee, I love him very much and we were planning to get married. I let him go, assuming that he would get over this craziness and return soon. So far, I have no word form him. Dr. Sonjee, you are a Hindu. Can you please tell me if he is coming back to me?"

THE MINISTER'S DAUGHTER

The day started just like every other day in my Las Vegas office. The schedule was not too busy, only five patients to see. I didn't have to go to the local hospital as I had no patients under my care. I had moved to Las Vegas in 1977 to start a psychiatric practice. I didn't come here because it was the gambling and entertainment capital of the world. I came instead because my friend Dr. Allen, an internist, had encouraged me to relocate to this desert city. He and I trained together in a large University Hospital Center in the Midwest. I found I liked the hot and dry climate of Las Vegas. My office was on Charleston Boulevard, not far from the Strip, the biggest tourist attraction in America with its hotels, casinos and places of entertainment. I wasn't much on gambling at the tables but I did enjoy playing the slot machines when I had time. Today I thought I would take off in the afternoon and play the machines at Harrah's Casino. With such pleasant thoughts I started seeing my patients, looking forward to the afternoon's break. I chuckled to myself as I thought about a supposedly respectable psychiatrist playing the slot machines, and further-more a Hindu of the Brahmin priest class. "Why not?" I said aloud.

About 1:30 my receptionist interrupted a session with a patient and informed me that I was to go to the hospital as soon as possible to examine a psy-chiatric emergency patient. I finished up with my patient and was on my way to the psychiatric ward, forgetting all about my plans to visit the Strip.

Miss Johnson, the RN on duty, was waiting for me. She said, "The patient was picked up near the Flamingo Hotel by the police. She was attempting to direct traffic on the Strip. Bystanders found her occasionally kneeling and praying in a loud voice and other times making obscene gestures to the crowd. She was combative when officers ap-proached her and she laughed at them and kicked them. We do not have any information on her back-ground. Her name is Anne Robertson. We had to put her in restraints and in an isolation room." Miss Johnson accompanied me to the room along with an aide, who unlocked the door and let me in first, then Miss Johnson followed. Miss Johnson intro-duced me to the patient, "Miss Robertson, this is Dr. Sonjee. He will be your psychiatrist."

I saw a young, thin, blond woman lying quietly in bed with eyes closed. I cautiously moved toward her and said, "Miss Robertson, I am Dr. Sonjee. I am a psychiatrist and I will help you." I waited for a response, but none was forthcoming. I gently asked her how she was feeling and what her thoughts were.

Again there was a pause and I waited. Miss Johnson interjected, "Please tell Dr. Sonjee what happened to you near the Flamingo Hotel." Suddenly there was an explosive response as the patient tried to wiggle out of the restraints and let go a torrent of profanity. Looking at me she screamed, "Dr. Sonjee, where are you from, India or Pakistan? What the hell are you doing in this country? Don't you have enough business in your own country? Then she turned towards Miss Johnson and said, "Look here, nurse, I do not want a foreign psychiatrist. Get me an American doctor." Miss Johnson, with an emphatic voice responded, "Dr. Sonjee is a very competent psychiatrist. He will be your doctor." The patient seemed to calm down and looked at me and asked, "What do you want to know?"

I repeated my questions with a gentle, reassuring voice and waited. There was a long pause and she was looking at the ceiling. She turned around and giggled and said, "I was told by God to direct traffic. Was there anything wrong with that?" I asked her how God directed her, did she hear God's voice? She said, "Yes, God told me to go out to the strip. You see my father is a Minister in Wyoming. I was raised a devout Christian. What are you Dr. Sonjee? A Hindu from India? Idol worshiper?" She giggled and after a minute said, "Why don't you let me out of these restraints and I will talk with you, Dr. Sonjee."

I told her I was going to start her on a series of intra-muscular medication as well as oral medications and said, "Within forty-eight hours you will be much improved and we'll talk then. In the meantime

I am leaving an order with the nursing staff to come in frequently and talk with you." As I was leaving the room she started a faint smile and then in the next moment she blasted me, "Dr. Sonjee, what a name, an Indian psychiatrist, God help me!" Miss Johnson and I left the seclusion room. I went to the nursing office to write orders and told Miss Johnson that I would come later in the evening to check on her.

About 9:00 PM I made it back to the hospital. I had a report that Miss Robertson was dozing off and on and seemed to be a bit more accessible to approach and not as unpredictable. I went to her room and said, "Miss Robertson, how are you feeling?" She opened her eyes and faintly said, "I am so sleepy. I am tired." I told her I'd see her in the morning.

The next day she was much improved. I ordered her restraints removed and out of seclusion, placed her on oral medications and told her I expected her to comply. I ordered a counselor for her and asked the nursing staff to encourage her to participate in all the activities. "Miss Robertson, you will be in the hospital for a few more days," I told her. "I will have a psychotherapy session with you tomorrow at 10 AM." She simply said, "Yes, I am better. Take it easy, Dr. Sonjee."

My session with her the next day was a complete assessment of her psychiatric syndrome. She related that she grew up in a troubled family. She was one of five daughters of a very prominent Baptist Minister. She gave a history of a regimented life, having to live up to the strict expectations of a minister's daughter. I found her to be a good historian with psychological insight. She stated that she had attended the University of Nevada at Las Vegas, but dropped out in her senior year. She took various low-paying jobs after that. She added, "I was very unhappy, stressed out, and I didn't know what to do with myself. I knew that I had failed my parents and felt I should die. I flunked out of the university, but I'm not dumb, Dr. Sonjee. I couldn't communicate with my parents and sisters. I knew I was in turmoil and that there was a storm slowly churning inside me."

I listened with patience as she delved into her past. Obviously she was in better contact with reality but occasionally she would have a far away look and giggle inappropriately. I said, "Please continue." She came out of her fantasies and continued, "I am now almost 24 and drifting rudderless in a sea which is stormy around me."

I was making meticulous notes so that I could have an understanding of her personality. She continued, " Just before I was brought to this hospital I cannot recall what happened to me. I suppose I snapped." I told her that she needed to be stabilized in the hospital for two more weeks and upon release she would have psychotherapy on a regular basis. She would also need to continue medications under the care of a psychiatrist. I felt that she was beginning to establish a rapport with me.

I saw her regularly in the hospital for brief sessions. At the time of her release I gave her the names of three other psychiatrists in Las Vegas, but she said she preferred to continue her treatment with me. I told her to call my office for an appointment and wrote her a prescription for her medications.

Our weekly sessions continued. It was a rocky road with ups and downs, some crises, but overall I thought she was making good progress. It must have been four months after her hospital release when she spontaneously brought up the episode of bizarre behavior just prior to her admission.

"You know, Dr. Sonjee, it is slowly coming back to me. At the time my mind was a blank. I am really ashamed to bring it up. Bits and pieces of that horrible night are intruding in my memory." I encouraged her by saying, "If you are ready, please go on, it is up to you." She stated, "Dr. Sonjee, after I dropped out of the University of Nevada I was on the verge of poverty with my minimum wage jobs. At one time I faced eviction and homelessness. One of my friends, Michelle, who also was a drop-out from the University, took me out to lunch. We shared some of our concerns and feelings and during the conversation she started telling me about an Escort Service in Las Vegas. She suggested I apply with them. For a moment it didn't register what that was about, but she explained that rich and lonely tourists come to Las Vegas and they look for companionship. I was stunned that my friend was suggesting that I join the oldest profession of mankind and become a prostitute. She told me about her experiences with the escort service called 'Alluring Ladies'. I became angry and was ready to walk out, but she held my hands and said, 'You do not know the dangers of homelessness in Las Vegas', and told me to call her if I wished. After finishing my shift at a restaurant I went home to my barely furnished apartment and started to cry. I needed a friend to reach out to me. I wanted my mother to be with me. Here I was in Las Vegas with all the glamour and excitement of an artificial world, alienated, and with homelessness staring me in the face. I thought about my friend's suggestion. I was not physically unattractive and I needed money to survive. I gingerly pulled out the Las Vegas telephone book and looked under 'Escort Service', in the yellow pages. There were dozens of entries under such fancy names as Enchanted Intentions, Raving Beauties, Valentine Escorts, City Nights, etc. It was difficult for me to imagine that I, the daughter of a minister, would turn to prostitution. The thought haunted me. I missed my mother but was unable to lift the phone to call her. Somehow I felt she was beyond my reach. I thought about my father, ministering to others, respected and loved in his small community, also beyond my reach. Financially life was getting tough. Apartment rent was due and I was facing eviction. I finally called my friend Michelle. She came over and we talked. She described her experiences in a non-threatening way. I was about to lift the cup of poison. I was about to forget all the sermons that I had heard growing up. Michelle understood my anxiety and fears. Despite her support I noticed a hint of tears in her eyes."

I interrupted her and asked, "What prevented you from calling your parents or simply returning home to stay with them for awhile?" She looked away and wiped her tears, "I really don't know. I felt I had failed them, that they were ashamed of me. There was an impassable sea between us. They are good folks and respected citizens, proud of what they have achieved in their lives. I didn't want a blemish on their reputation. I knew one of my sisters, now in Detroit, was deep into substance abuse. My parents conveniently denied it. I knew they loved me but their love was not enough to surmount their pride and reputation. Does that make sense?"

I told her to proceed in telling me about the meeting with Michelle. "Yes, Michelle hugged me and we both cried. She told me that she'd introduce me to the people at 'Alluring Ladies' the next day. I had a restless night. I had nightmares about my father. The next morning I thought I should run away or jump in front of a car. Anyway, I got dressed and looked in the mirror. I didn't look the same. I closed all the windows and started sobbing and all I could say was, 'Oh Mom, Oh Mom'."

"Why didn't you call your mother then?" I asked. She got up from her chair and screamed at me, "You psychiatrists, don't you have a heart? All these probing questions." I remained quiet. She started sobbing again and said, "I was not quite honest with you when I told you why I didn't return to my parents' home." She again became agitated, proceeded towards the door and screamed at me, "Dr. Sonjee, I want a female psychiatrist. You are not supportive. This is too much."

Again I stayed calm and quiet. She returned to her chair, stopped sobbing and looked straight at me and said, "You Hindus believe in destiny and Karma. I suppose what happened to me was my destiny."

I responded, "Is there something you would like to share with me?" She got up from the chair, looked out the window and stated from there, "I don't want to drag my Minister father into this, and my memory is rather unclear. Do you think it could be a distortion of my mind?"

"I don't quite get it", I said.

She proceeded, "I have had frequent nightmares about my father. I think I must have been about seven or eight." She started crying again as if she wouldn't stop. I waited. "I have a vague memory that my father was trying to molest me." She stopped at this point and remained mute, with a far-away look as if she weren't there. She continued after awhile. "He made numerous attempts at touching and fondling me, all in the name of fatherly love. My pleas to him to stop were in vain. Finally I told him that unless he stopped I would go before the congregation and make a plea to them. He must have seen the fire in my eyes. Dr. Sonjee, this is too painful, I want to get back to talking about my experience with 'Alluring Ladies'. That evening I was to meet my first tourist. Michelle called me up with a word of encouragement. I met him in the lobby of a hotel on the Strip. He was a foreign tourist, perhaps from Europe. We went to dinner, had a few drinks, although I only had one. Then I accompanied him to his room in a very classy hotel. When we arrived in the room I went into the bathroom to undress, as expected. I was very nervous and I started to cry. I put my hands around my chest and said 'Oh Mother'. Then I locked the door to the bathroom and then sat on the floor and started sobbing loudly. Soon there was a knock on the door. I ignored it but the knock became persistent. I got up, completely naked, and opened the door to be confronted by a naked, obese, middle-aged man who was pointing a handgun at me. With the gun he motioned me to move toward the bed. I panicked as I saw two leather straps and a knife so I jumped at him. We both fell on the floor as I struggled with him to deflect the gun away from me. I felt so abnormally strong. I saw that he was panting and puffing and I soon was able to get the gun from him. I firmly directed him to lie on the floor and warned him that I would shoot him if I heard any noise or saw any movement. I never saw a more frightened man. I went to the bathroom, keeping the door open, and got dressed in a hurry. I've never had any experience with a gun and I wouldn't have known how to fire it, but I kept it pointed towards him. I came out, saw a hundred dollar bill on the floor and picked it up and threw it at him. He face was terror-stricken and he was speechless. I walked backwards towards the door, still pointing the gun at him, opened the door, and then placed the gun on a table and said, 'I was raised as a good Christian girl and I forgive you.' When I got home I called Michelle right away and she came over and we hugged and cried. I reflected on the fact that I was about to enter the profession and about to kill a man. I became obsessed with it. It was as if the hand of God was protecting me. After Michelle left I started praying and singing all the hymns I remembered from childhood. I hardly slept that night. I think I was hearing voices. I do not recall my behavior that afternoon on the Strip near the Flamingo Hotel, but you know that story."

I listened to this stunning story in rapt attention.

There were many more sessions with her in the months that followed where we dealt with a number of issues. She did well in supporting herself by working two jobs. She no longer needed psychiatric medication. She was even attempting to re-establish her relationship with her family. After a year we mutually decided to terminate therapy sessions. Her plan at that point was to re-enter the University of Nevada at Las Vegas to finish her degree and then enter the Masters in Social Work program. Her ultimate goal was to work with neglected and abused children. On her last session she thanked me for sticking with her. She was very beautiful and quite gracious in her remarks.

I declined to take any credit and said to her half-jokingly, "We Hindus believe in Destiny and Karma." I opened the door for her and she shook my hand. I came back to the second floor window of my office where I could look down onto the parking lot and saw her walking towards her car. She looked up to the window before entering her car and waved a good-bye and I waved back.

In the Winter of 1984 I was in Reno, Nevada for a psychiatric conference. There were hundreds of participants. It was at a dinner meeting with speakers talking about post-traumatic stress disorder that I caught the glance of a woman at the next table. She was quite beautiful. I was sure it was Anne Robertson, my former patient from Las Vegas. I was anxious for a break in the session so I could speak with her. I approached her, gave her my business card, and asked if I could see her after the session. She smiled and nodded. I waited in the lobby for her. She soon came and warmly shook my hand. We chatted for a few minutes. Anne had indeed completed her Masters in Social Work and was working with abused and neglected children and their families. She said she was very focused on the work she was doing, and was still single. She did re-establish a relationship with her parents and sisters, although it was a distant one. I felt there was a bit of tension and nervousness when we talked. There was a period of silence and I said, "Anne, would you like to go to dinner with me tomorrow evening and maybe see a show afterwards?" There was a pause and then suddenly she laughed aloud and she could hardly stop. I too started laughing, not knowing what to expect. Finally she said, "I am sorry Dr. Sonjee, I just didn't expect this from you." She smiled and said, "Do you think I am crazy to go on a date with a psychiatrist, and especially a Hindu psychiatrist?"

I laughed and then she added in a more serious tone, "Really, don't you think it is unethical to date a patient, Dr. Sonjee?"

I said, "Yes, a patient, but not a former patient from years ago."

She squeezed my hand and said, "I will think about it. Why don't you give me a call around 10:00 tomorrow morning?". With that she jotted down her hotel and room number. She stood up and gave me a kiss on my cheek. While walking away she stopped for a moment, and laughingly shouted back, "Dr. Sonjee, am I an alluring lady?"

THE PALE MOON OVER SAMBALPUR

I received the following mysterious letter from India one fine afternoon in Dallas, Texas. Being a very busy psychiatrist it oftentimes would take me days to catch up with my mail.

Sometimes I would get letters from people in India that I didn't know. However, this letter was unusual. It said:

> 10 January 1984
> Quarter No. B/366
> Sector-35, Rourkela 769006
> India

Dear Doctor Sonjee:

I do not think you will remember me. You and I grew up in Sambalpur. I lived in Jharuapara. You were one year junior to me in High School. You and I and other friends used to go swimming in the Mahanadi when it was in flood. You came from a poor family. Luckily for me my family owned land and had a business. You might not remember but I used to buy you snacks from my daily allowance. I am not saying this to make you feel bad, but I am just trying to jog your memory about me. I became an Engineer and am now retired in Rourkela. I think of you often and have treasured my friendship with you. You were almost like my younger brother. I hear that you are about to make a vacation trip to India. I would like you to do one thing for me. Would you stop in England and do a project for me? My grandfather was a petty revenue agent under the British Government around 1914 in Sambalpur. A British officer named John Lucas had gone tiger hunting near Mundher in Sambalpur district. He had taken a large number of followers with him on this tiger hunt. My grandfather was one of them. The hunting lodge is still there, though it is in partial ruins. I was not even born yet but as a boy in Sambalpur I witnessed my grandmother crying almost weekly in a corner in our courtyard. It went on for years. She never shared what she was crying about. She never complained. From the vague information I heard as a boy my grandfather was accidentally shot by John Lucas in that hunting expedition. His body was brought to the hunting lodge and finally transported to Sambalpur by bullock cart, arriving in the early morning at Jharuapada. It was still dark with a pale moon shining over Sambalpur. I heard that my grandmother passed out and remained in bed for six months. My father was about sixteen and my aunt about five. I will not bore you further about my family but I wondered if you would find out in England what happened to John Lucas. I realize it is almost seventy years ago that this tragedy happened, leaving my grandmother a widow with small children. My father never talked about it. Maybe I am insane to be obsessed with something that happened seventy years ago but the wounds inflicted on our family have never healed. Will you please stop in London, do research at the British Government's India Office Library and Records, trace John Lucas and find out what happened to him? I know it is a tall order. My grandmother and father are now gone. Who knows how much they suffered. The memory of my friendship with you is a strong as ever. I cherish that memory. I leave this matter to you. With my best wishes I remain,

Narayan Panda

I thought it was a strange letter. During my long walks I began to remember Narayan. I recalled my childhood days in Sambalpur, swimming in the Mahanadi, the colorful festivals of Sambalpur, long walks after school hours, visits to the temples, and above all best friends whose memories lie deep in my heart, friends who are there and those who have departed. Slowly I began to recall Narayan and the activities we shared in our school days. Despite this friendship of days gone by I thought this request was bizarre, but the story fascinated me. I decided to stop in England for a few days and pursue this story. I replied to Narayan that I would do this for him and report to him at Rourkela.

It was spring time in London when I arrived, such a beautiful time of the year. I had been to London before, thus my single mission was to find out about John Lucas. The next morning I was at the India Office Library and Records on Blackfriars Road as soon as the doors opened. I inquired about the information I was seeking and was referred to Jane Davenport, who was a specialist on India matters and specifically the prestigious cadre of Indian Civil Service to which John Lucas belonged. Miss Davenport took me to her small office and I told her what I was seeking. She was a small woman with thick glasses and a frozen smile, a bit nervous with a fine tremor in her right hand. She asked me, "Dr. Sonjee, do you have any other information about John Lucas, such as his place and date of birth, and the year he went to India?"

"No, Miss Davenport", I said, "You might look up Indian Civil Service in the Province of Bihar and Orissa in 1914. Sambalpur District was a part of it."

She asked me to accompany her to a section of the Library which had indexed information regarding Indian Civil Service. She quickly found a small card on John Lucas with the following information: "Lucas, John M. Born August 29, 1891, Indian Civil Service 1913. Served in Sambalpur District 1913-15, Patna District 1915-19, Singhbhum District 1920-25, Joint Secretary, Revenue Department 1925-29, Education Secretary 1930-33, Revenue Commissioner 1934-39, Additional Chief Secretary, 1940-43, Chief Secretary, 1944-47. Retired from the Indian Civil Service, August, 1947. Settled in his ancestral home,

27 James Street, Edinburgh, Scotland. Died February 15, 1963. Survived by his daughter Elizabeth Lucas."

With the professionalism of a librarian Miss Davenport jotted down all of the information on a card and handed it to me. I thanked her profusely and as I was ready to depart she placed her hand on my arm and said in a timid voice, "Dr. Sonjee, John Lucas was born almost a century ago and served in India so many years back   I'm curious about your interest in this bit of history. What caused you, an Indian American, to seek information on him?" I sat down and told her the whole story of my mission. She asked me what I planned to do next and I said that I would be on my way to Edinburgh to talk with Miss Lucas. She wished me good luck, but shook her heads sideways a few times, almost implying that I might be a bit insane to pursue something like this story.

Early the next morning I was on the express train to Edinburgh. What wonderful countryside with vistas of absolutely beautiful landscapes! Rolling hills and meadows, small English villages, occasionally a castle, a witness to some colorful or tragic event in English history. I thought about the people who were restless and adventurous and had wandered the world for almost three centuries accumulating land until they had an Empire on which the sun never set. It was a 375-mile trip through this dream country. All of this seemed a bit unreal, a train journey through this beautiful countryside in search of a daughter of a man I never knew.

I arrived at Waverley Train Station around four in the afternoon and took a taxi to a room and board facility on James Street. I went in the lobby and encountered a matronly Scottish lady who said I was fortunate to find a room. I had dinner and soon fell asleep.

The next morning, after breakfast I walked on James Street until I came to a small, quaint house marked No. 27. A lovely garden decorated the front yard. I was a bit nervous. I knocked on the door and heard footsteps. A small lady with pale white skin, blondish hair and no make-up opened the door. At first she seemed suspicious, perhaps quizzical, and before I could say anything, she quipped, in broken Hindi, "Ap Kon Hey?", which might mean "Who are you?" Obviously she knew I was from India. I laughed aloud, not expecting Hindi from this British lady. My laughter caused a scowl on her face and she waited. I began calmly, "Miss Lucas, I am sorry I've appeared on your doorstep unannounced. You see, I was born in Sambalpur where your father served as an officer around 1914." That was all I could utter before she transformed into a smiling, warm person, welcoming me into her living room, chattering away in half-Hindi, half-English, much of which was incomprehensible to me. She had me sit down on a sofa, brought tea and biscuits and kept on talking about her days in India. She frequently referred to Patna and was obviously reminiscing about her life in India.

After a time she realized that I must have had a purpose for being at her home and she said, "I am sorry, what is your name and why are you here? I sort of got carried away when I saw you, an Indian. You know I love India. I wish I had not returned to this awful climate of Scotland. Tell me, do you know how to cook? How I do love those Indian curries." Again, she drifted into her own memories and seemed to forget that I was there. I let her talk. It was most fascinating. Finally she sat down close to me and again asked me my name and purpose of the visit.

"Miss Lucas," I said, "I got your name and address from the India Office Library and Records in London. You see I am here on a mission." Then I proceeded to tell her briefly about myself and my friend's request. She was listening carefully. She didn't respond right away and her expression became serious. She went to the kitchen to get more tea and biscuits and when she returned she told me an extraordinary story. She talked for a long time, non-stop. At times she was tearful, at other times she appeared agitated. She spoke clearly and coherently.

"Dr. Sonjee, I always had a fear that someone from India would come here to ask me about my father. Maybe I was hoping it would happen so that I could get this haunting incident out of my mind. Let me tell you a little about myself. I was born in Patna in 1929. My mother died in childbirth. My father decided to raise me by himself with the help of those wonderful Ayahas that you have in your country. They were like my own mother. My father never remarried. The English custom then was to send the children to boarding schools in England, but father decided not to do that, and enrolled me in St. Andrews School in Patna. I had wonderful friends, both Indian and European. You see I was a bit spoiled with all the servants. Dr. Sonjee, have you been to Patna? The British used to go picnicking on the banks of the Ganges. My father was a big officer, something like a Secretary to the Government. I was the apple of his eye. He didn't like club activities and devoted much of his time to work. Perhaps he was lonely. Have you been to the British cemetery in Patna? My mother is buried there. I can only remember how sad my father was at times. He missed my mother. Other than that I was so happy. By the by, where are you staying Dr. Sonjee? You must move here to my house tomorrow. We have more to talk about. Also you must cook some curry for me. Yes, Patna is such a wonderful place. My mama is there."

I didn't feel like interrupting her. I could see that talking about her past was a catharsis. I sat quietly listening. She continued, "When I was about sixteen or so I heard from a friend of mine that my father had accidentally shot and killed someone on a tiger hunt in Sambalpur. Yes, my friend's name was Mary Duncan. Now after seventy years you come to see me in Edinburgh with this story. I heard exactly what your friend wrote to you in his letter. It was accidental. I never confronted my father about this and he never shared anything about it in India. My father decided to retire and leave India in 1947 when your country became independent. I hated to leave India. I had finished high school, but all my friends were there. I hadn't known any other country except India. India has her own charm. Your mother

India is truly like a mother." At this point Miss Lucas started weeping. I remained silent. I thought about two hundred years of British rule in India and how the British developed a special relationship with India. Miss Lucas composed herself soon and continued her story. "It was fall when we returned to this country and my father was keen that I enroll in the University of Edinburgh. We came to this house. You know, this house has been with our family since 1727. My father was the only child of his parents. While here my father remained seclusive. He did not attend clubs for folks who had returned from India, where they constantly talk about India. Life went on. I took care of my father and managed all the household affairs. Then in the summer of 1962 my father became severely depressed. He became even more of a recluse. He wouldn't eat at times. His sleep became disturbed. He lost interest in his usual activities. At times he would sob in his room. He began to have nightmares. He wouldn't share his thoughts and feelings with me. Obviously he needed psychiatric care. I think you told me you have been a psychiatrist in America. I took him to our family doctor. He was placed on medications of one kind or another, then sent to a psychiatric hospital for several weeks. Sometimes he would mutter words in Hindi, at other times he would carry on an imaginary conversation in mixed English and another language of India, maybe the language of Sambalpur. It took a long time for me to figure out that he was talking with his victim in Sambalpur. His name was something like Madhusudan.

I interrupted Miss Lucas to ask if she could recall the content of the conversation. She simply said, "I can only recall some phrases such as 'Madhusudan, I didn't mean it. You know that'."

I asked her, "How did he act when he was carrying on this conversation?"

She paused for a moment and added, "He was like a tiger in a cage, pacing back and forth in the room, totally oblivious that I was around."

I gently asked her, "Did you understand what the victim, Madhusudan, was telling your father?"

She replied, "My father would sometimes quote the victim's replies with a mix of English and another language, I think of Orissa, in his imaginary conversation. I remember my father saying that a voice used to speak to him and it said, 'Sahib, I left a widow with two children. My oldest son is only sixteen. How is he going to support the family?' and my father would scream back at the imaginary voice, 'Stop saying this to me over and over. We gave your son a job in our office'." I asked her how he would behave when this happened. She said, "After the illusionary conversation,he would become exhausted and on one occasion I heard his muttering to himself, 'Oh God, I should have gone to console the widow and her children. We British are so prudish'!"

I gently changed the subject and asked her, "Did he talk about Sambalpur?"

"Oh yes", she said. "He talked of Sambalpur many times. He referred to the river you have there, I forgot the name."

"The Mahanadi," I added.

She continued, "I often attempted to find out from him what was bothering him deep down. I had an idea that he might be re-living the emotional trauma and pain of that homicide, even though it was accidental. His condition continued to decline. I was able to take care of him at home in spite of the hallucinations and the imaginary conversations. Sometimes I would hear him shout, 'Oh God forgive me'. Still he wouldn't share any details with me. Shall we take a pause?"

It was about noon. She added, "I have some potato and peas curry. I can warm it up. It is not like the wonderful curries of Patna, but perhaps you'll enjoy it. How I wish I had some of your mangoes."

She left to prepare lunch, leaving me alone with my thoughts, I admired her, a strong woman from the past with one foot in India and another in Scotland. Thinking of her being motherless at birth saddened me, but I knew she was given love and affection from the ayahas. She returned in a few minutes and asked me to accompany her to a small dining room. The view was spectacular and before sitting down for lunch she pointed out the top of the Holyrood Abbey, a historical landmark in Edinburgh. Miss Lucas was a meticulous homemaker. On the walls of the dining room were several paintings of Indian scenes, including one of the Ganges River in Patna. She started chatting about all the various dishes that the British were fond of in India. After lunch we returned to the living room and she resumed the memories of her father.

"Dr. Sonjee, my father suffered a lot. He was rarely coherent and happy, but when he was he would tell stories about his wonderful life in India, and about my mother. Mostly he was profoundly sad, and then occasionally he would carry on this imaginary conversation with the accident victim in Sambalpur.

"Miss Lucas, did he ever share any details about the victim?" I asked. Miss Lucas excused herself and brought an old, faded photograph. She handed it to me. It was a street scene in India. It could have been any town in that big country. I waited for her to speak. She said, "My father once told me that this is a street in Sambalpur. The victim's family lived in a lane off this main street. He had a wife and two children, a boy of sixteen, and a girl of five." I asked, "Are you sure he didn't visit the widow and the children?" Miss Lucas referred to the imaginary conversation and suggested that he probably did not as in those days the British didn't mix with the Indians." She added, "My friend, Mary Duncan, told me that the British tried to keep the incident quiet. Her father was the District Inspector of Police and according to him it was clearly a case of negligent homicide. You know that when the British ruled India they had a different set of laws for themselves."

I interjected, "You mean they were beyond the laws they made for Indians."

She replied, "It seems so."

I asked Miss Lucas how he died and if she thought he was tormented by guilt the rest of his life. "Yes he was," she sobbed and asked me to accompany her to the basement of her home. I didn't know what to expect. She seemed agitated and tearful. She held my hand as the basement was dimly lit. She pointed to a hook on the ceiling and said, "In the evening of February 16, 1963 1 found him dead hanging from there by a rope." Then she collapsed into my arms and started sobbing like a young girl. It must have been several minutes before she regained her composure.

We returned to the living room. I was exhausted from the emotion of the story. I had been with Miss Lucas for several hours now. I asked her where her father was buried.

She answered, "In the yard of the St. Bernard's Church, I visit his grave frequently. Would you like to come with me?"

"Yes I would," I said.

On our way to the cemetery she bought two bouquets of flowers. It was getting a bit dark and there was a pale moon in the sky. Once inside the cemetery I followed her quietly. There were hundreds of graves in the yard of the old church, some dating back several hundred years.

Finally Miss Lucas stopped in front of a grave. She placed her bouquet on the grave and then asked me to do the same. When I read the words on the gravestone I couldn't help shedding a few tears myself. We held hands and stood in silence for a minute.

We returned to her home and I thanked Miss Lucas for the time she spent with me and all for the information. I gave her a hug and told her I was on my way to India for a visit. As she wiped a tear from her face, I realized that here was a woman who had left her heart in India.

In March of 1984, when I went to Rourkela I visited with my friend Narayan. We had much to talk about besides our childhood days in Sambalpur. Narayan was patient and I knew he wanted to hear what I had found out in England. When the time was appropriate I told him what I had found out about John Lucas. I held my friend's hands and said, "Narayan, John Lucas is buried in a cemetery in the St. Bernard's Church yard in Edinburgh. I visited the grave with his daughter, Elizabeth, and the grave-stone had only one sentence engraved, 'Oh God forgive me'. It is time for you to forgive also and forget."

THE PEEPAL TREE

Ohio was experiencing one of the most bitter winters that anyone could remember. Columbus was blanketed with snow. The sky was overcast. There had been no sun for days. It was very depressing weather.

Dr. Sonjee has been in practice of psychiatry for many years. After completing his training in a reputable mid-western University Medical Center, he decided to locate in Columbus. He enjoyed the many cultural events and programs offered by Ohio State University. Despite the weather, his day was full with appointments.

"Dr. Sonjee, you are a Hindu. You are a shrink in America. Is that compatible? You Hindus believe in millions of Gods and Goddesses. You even believe in a God of Death, Yama or something like that. You believe in ghosts and witches. Don't take me wrong, Doc. I am your patient here in this hospital. There is nothing personal against you. Besides, I am curious."

Dr. Sonjee interrupted his patient in this psychotherapeutic session, and asked, "Mr. Girod, are you expressing concerns about my competency to understand and treat you?"

"No," Mr. Girod replied, "Nothing like that, Doc. I like you personally. It's just that I have been to so many psychiatrists for my mental problems. Maybe a Hindu psychiatrist can fix me. With all the mystery and magic of your religion, you may have special powers."

Mr. Girod was a bright, likeable patient who suffered from anxiety attacks, intense headaches, outbursts against family members, whom he loved dearly, and varying periods when he would withdraw from the world. Being a relatively wealthy man, he had gone to a number of psychiatrists and psychoanalysts while living in Detroit. His symptoms waxed and waned, but he never became stabilized.

Dr. Sonjee and Mr. Girod had had a good therapeutic rapport, but today's discussion disturbed Dr. Sonjee. He wondered about Mr. Girod's comments. His reference to ghosts and witches specially bothered him. The encounter with Mr. Girod made Dr. Sonjee think of Samantapur.

Samantapur was an ancient little town in the heart of India, situated on the bank of a sacred and turbulent river. While taking daily walks in the streets of Columbus, Dr. Sonjee would think about his upbringing in a traditional society, his religion and the rituals, and the many temples of Samantapur. Somehow, the temple to Shiva, the Hindu God of Destruction, intruded again and again on his consciousness. It has been many years since he last visited the temple, but all the images were sharp. At first, he couldn't understand why he would be preoccupied with the temple for so many days in Columbus, so far away from Samantapur. There were multiple flashes of memory, the temple with the sacred Peepal tree in the backyard and on the bank of the river. He knew that his father had regularly worshipped Shiva in the temple. That night he felt anxious and apprehensive.

Dr. Sonjee had a restless night. It must have been the early hours of the morning that he heard himself mumbling, waking up with a sense of fear but with great relief that it was only a dream about the ghost in the Peepal tree. The people of Samantapur, he pondered with much fondness, were so hopelessly superstitious. They had their beliefs in the magic, the mysterious and above all, in ghosts and witches. He smiled to himself. But the ghost in the Peepal tree was unique. He remembered that as a child he had heard that a highly respected and beloved teacher had died rather suddenly while only in his late twenties. His death had shocked the ancient town. Nobody could remember the details. It was many years since he had passed away, but all Samantapur still believed that his ghost had taken abode in the Peepal tree along with other ghosts.

Dr. Sonjee remembered, as a child, all the stories about the Peepal tree, about all the ghosts living there, and their nocturnal wanderings in Samantapur. Above all, he remembered the Teacher Ghost, who according to old-timers died an unhappy man because of a romance that had failed and broke his heart. The story was that he was dead for at least three days before the neighbors became concerned because nobody had seen him or his elderly mother. When some town elders from Samantapur broke into the house, they found the old woman cradling her son on her lap, softly talking to him and telling him to 'Wake Up'. Nobody knew how he died. The old woman sobbed loudly every night and never accepted that her son was gone. She died a few months later.

It was almost two years later that Dr. Sonjee visited Samantapur. Even though his visit was a whirl-wind of activities, he thought about the nightmarish dream in Columbus, about the Peepal tree and the Teacher-Ghost who had paid a visit to him. Although the ghost was a vague and blurred image in his mind, nevertheless on this brief visit to Samantapur, he was keenly aware of that image. As time passed, he began to ask himself, "Why not visit with the Teacher-Ghost? Why not find out what happened to him? Why not find out if that Ghost even existed in that Peepal Tree? Why not find out how he died an untimely death? Why not find out what his mother had told him just before he passed away? Why not—?" All those questions began to agitate him. He wondered if he was losing his mind. After all he was a psychiatrist.

It was almost midnight. Dr. Sonjee couldn't sleep. He looked at the immobile lizard on the ceiling of that guest house in Samantapur. It was drizzling outside. He opened the window and looked out, anxiously. Samantapur, the town where he grew up, slept, still with hardly any sounds, unlike his town in distant America. He got dressed, went out of the guest house, started walking towards the temple and the Peepal tree. It was probably a mile or so. The street was lighted dimly. He didn't see anyone. It was safe to walk alone in Samantapur even at that time of night, unlike many towns in America. He could see some people sleeping on cots on the street, others on verandas adjoining their houses.

The narrow street leading to the temple of Lord Shiva, the Hindu God of Destruction, had no lights at all, so he walked slowly. As a child, he had walked that street many times on his way to the river. He was a bit surprised that he was not anxious, but rather expectant and curious. He slowly went around the ancient temple to the backyard. He didn't see anything or hear anything. He looked around, went even closer to the Peepal tree. It was so dark. He slowly went forward and touched the tree with reverence. A flood of memories came back to him. He thought of his many visits to this ancient temple, and the people of Samantapur who had long since departed. He felt like he had gone back in a time tunnel. He began to feel anxious, thought it was time to return to the guest house when he heard a clear voice, "Come near me. I have been waiting for you for fifty some years."

Startled, Dr. Sonjee suddenly felt frightened. He thought he was hallucinating, but managed to say simply, "Who are you?"

"I am the Teacher-Ghost. I visited you in your dream at Columbus. Do you remember what I had told you to do?" Dr. Sonjee took courage and said clearly, "Yes, it just came back to me. You directed me to come and visit you. I can even remember your face in that dream. Here I am, all the way from

America." He looked around. He didn't see or hear any apparition, no movement or sounds after what seemed like an eternity. Then he heard the same voice coming from the top of the tree, "I will tell you my story. People in Samantapur think that I died very unhappy, and that is why my soul is not liberated and that is why I became a Ghost. They even think I was either murdered or killed myself. I want you to know the truth."

Dr. Sonjee looked up into the rustling tree branches. He found himself shouting at the tree "Tell me the truth."

"I will tell you the truth. Do you remember the well only a few yards from my house? Perhaps you have forgotten, but it is about a quarter of a mile from here. I have visited that well every night since I have given up my body."

Dr. Sonjee shouted again, demandingly, "Please go on."

"Yes, that well from which her body was recovered. People in Samantapur have forgotten her, but not me."

Dr. Sonjee protested, "No, I haven't forgotten. Her name was Basanti. She was extraordinarily beautiful and you were in love with her."

He heard a deep sigh not too far from where he was standing.

"Yes, I was in love with her, and she was in love with me. it was 1927. But we were not allowed to get married."

Dr. Sonjee spoke back, "Basanti committed suicide." He looked up into the tree again, still failing to see anything.

A sad voice came back, "Yes, she jumped into that well. They found her body the next morning."

Dr. Sonjee replied, "My mind is playing tricks on me. I was then a small boy. I cannot remember all my feelings. I didn't understand why Basanti had to kill herself. Please accept my heartfelt sympathy, but why couldn't you get married?"

"Dr. Sonjee, you have been away in America too long. Don't you remember all the taboos, the caste system and no marriage between castes. You know I was a Brahmin and Basanti belonged to a low caste. All of Samantapur was against our marriage. I pleaded with the citizens of Samantapur. It all fell on deaf ears. Basanti and I became the target of ridicule, hatred and taunts. Life became unbearable for us. There were only two people who supported us, and that was my mother and your father."

Dr. Sonjee heard a resounding laughter from the top of the Peepal tree, "My mother, what a woman! I can tell you how progressive she was, supporting her Brahmin son for a love marriage with a girl of lower caste, a thing unheard of anywhere in India in those days. I would say my mother and your father belonged to the next century in their progressive thinking and acceptance of all human beings."

Dr. Sonjee interrupted, "Get on with the story and nothing but the truth."

"After Basanti's death, I became a recluse. I wouldn't come out of the house. Once I tried, but was hit with stones. I decided that I should meet Death. You know the Sufis of ancient India, almost like sages and gurus, men of much wisdom. They used to decide on the time of their departure from this world. You should read the stories of the great Sufis of Delhi during the days of Sultanate, before the Moguls conquered India. I made an appointment with Death and entered into deep meditation."

Dr. Sonjee couldn't keep himself screaming at the treetop, "Go on! What was it like, your tryst with Death?"

The voice came back clearly, "I remained in deep peace. I meditated on the great philosophical questions of life, as the sages had done for thousands of years. I was enlightened. I was no more an earthly creature, but somewhere else. I died on my mother's lap. I had invited Death, it wasn't suicide. You tell the people of Samantapur my true story. I have to leave now."

Dr. Sonjee shouted back, "Do not leave. I have one question, you must answer."

He heard the voice, "Go ahead."

"Why did you wait for so long to tell your story? And why did you call me all the way from America to tell your story? You could have told your story to someone else in Samantapur."

Dr. Sonjee looked up into the tree again, straining his ears for the voice to come back. After a long pause, the voice came back, clear and compassionate, "I am glad you ask that question. I had almost forgotten to tell you the rest. Not very far from you on your left, in the temple courtyard, the bier with your father's body was brought in. You know very well that he died suddenly after a brief illness just after you left for America. I remember that night. The entire town was in shock, almost in disbelief that he had passed away. You know those ancient Hindu rites for twelve days before a soul is released. Those rites for your father were held very close to this tree, and I was a witness to all of those rites."

Dr. Sonjee felt dizzy, he felt his heart pounding against his chest wall but he shouted back, "Tell me more, tell me all, tell me the truth, the whole story".

The voice came back, soothing and calming, "Before his soul was released on the twelfth day, he came and talked with me."

"Do you mean that his apparition came and talked with you? Do you mean to say he came to talk with you after he passed away?"

The voice clearly replied, "Yes, he came to this tree. He told me to give this message to you, 'My son is on his way to America. Some people in Samantapur are saying that I died because of the shock at his departure. You call him for a visit, tell him your story and tell him what I have told you just now. And give him this family ring to take to America. And with that, your father handed me a gold ring."

Dr. Sonjee stood there overwhelmed with emotions, until he felt a ring slip into his palm.

It was getting to be almost early dawn. He looked at the ring which his father had once worn, and then he looked up at the tree. It was just a beautiful old Peepal tree slowly emerging into the light of the dawn. He stood there with folded hands, and softly said "Thank you."

On his way back to the guest house, he stopped at the well, looked down, and offered a silent prayer.

It had been many years since his return from India. He was busy seeing patients in his office in Columbus. During an interlude, his receptionist called him, and said, "A Mr. Girod would like to see you for a few minutes." Dr. Sonjee clearly remembered his patient, Mr. Girod who had improved very much, and was now a successful travel agent in Detroit.

Dr. Sonjee came out quickly to the reception area and greeted Mr. Girod warmly, and guided him into his office. Mr. Girod, Dr. Sonjee noticed, looked healthy and well. He talked about his family and business and a recent trip to India. He told Dr. Sonjee how much he enjoyed his visit to India. After a lot of friendly conversation, Dr. Sonjee suddenly remembered what Mr. Girod had said about him being a Hindu, believing in Gods and Goddesses, ghosts and witches. He reminded Mr. Girod about it.

Mr. Girod laughingly said, "Well Doc, do you still believe in Gods and Goddesses, ghosts and witches after being in America for so many years?"

Dr. Sonjee became tense, went over to the window, and then returned to his chair. Mr. Girod noticed that Dr. Sonjee had a faraway look, as if in another world. He added, "Sorry, Doc, perhaps I offended you."

Dr. Sonjee quickly said, "Not at all, Mr. Girod. I just thought about a ghost, an encounter with a friendly ghost, shall we say." Both of them laughed aloud, and then, Dr. Sonjee looked fondly at the gold ring he was wearing on the middle finger of his right hand.

THE QUEEN OF BHUBANESWAR

It was 1983 that Minneapolis was experiencing an extremely hot summer. It was almost like the hot summers of Orissa, that beautiful state on the Bay of Bengal in India, where Dr. Sonjee came from. He had been a very busy psychiatrist in Minneapolis for almost twenty-five years. Today, he was restless, perhaps due to the heat, or more perhaps, due to homesickness, loneliness and may be psychological burn-out resulting from intense involvement with mental patients on a daily basis. His mind frequently would wander to his childhood days in a small and colorful town in Orissa. He would daydream about a stroll on the beach at Puri or having a quiet weekend at Gopalpur-on-Sea. At times, a fleeting memory of a departed boyhood friend would haunt his mind and his heart would cry out in pain.

He had two more patient appointments and after that, he went on a long walk inside the beautiful campus of the University of Minnesota, which was not too far away from his office on Como Avenue.

On his return home, Dr. Sonjee quickly went through his mail and was pleasantly surprised to have a letter from his nephew, Ajit, in Bhubaneswar. Ajit had invited Dr. Sonjee to stay in Bhubaneswar for several days during his upcoming trip to India.

Bhubaneswar is the new capital of Orissa, but the city's history goes back to perhaps twenty-five hundred years. The city is dominated by the great temple of Lord Shiva, the Lingaraj Temple, completed in the eleventh century AD. Just a few miles from the city is the Jain rock cave complex dating back to the second century BC. Also nearby is the River Daya. Legend has it that it became a river of blood after the great battle won by the invading Emperor Ashoka against the army of Orissa. Nearby is the Dhauli complex with the Emperor's rock edicts. It was from here that Ashoka set out on his mission of spreading Buddhism.

How can Dr. Sonjee decline a visit to Bhubaneswar? From the sizzling hot summer of Minneapolis, Bhubaneswar appeared to be an ideal place to stay for a few days. He thought, during his stay there, he would visit the Lingaraj Temple daily, offer prayers to Lord Shiva just like his fore-fathers had done. He would revisit the jewels of temples: the Rajarani and the Mukteswar. In Khandagiri and Udayagiri, he would listen to the voices coming out of these great architectural masterpieces.

It was December 1983 when Dr. Sonjee arrived at Bhubaneswar. Ajit and his family were there to meet him at the airport. Dr. Sonjee was momentarily overwhelmed with the genuine warmth and joy that pervaded the scene. Ajit, as usual, was beaming with smiles. Soon thereafter, Ajit escorted his uncle to the Kalinga Ashok, a fairly modern hotel in Gautam Nagar.

Dr. Sonjee planned his days well: visits to temples, the caves and occasionally, simply wandering around in Bhubaneswar, transporting himself in his fantasies to those years in history when the city boasted of some thousand temples. He even pictured himself as an ascetic going from one temple to another, chanting prayers to Lord Shiva.

Ajit suggested one evening that they go to the Pushpanjali, the elegant restaurant in the Oberoi. This was not an unwelcome break from Dr. Sonjee's fascination with what Bhubaneswar was. Dr. Sonjee liked the decor of the restaurant, with large paintings on the walls of the great temples of Orissa, soft classical music and the aroma of freshly cooked foods. Food was ordered, Dr. Sonjee preferring South Indian delicacies, such as Upama and Masala Dosha. It was a very pleasant atmosphere, with good food and light talk with his nephew. Dr. Sonjee could hardly think of Minneapolis.

All of a sudden, the restaurant door opened and there was a babble of excited voices and in walked a stunningly beautiful lady followed by at least two dozens of persons of both sexes. Dr. Sonjee almost mumbled to himself, "Most beautiful eyes, long dark silken hair, elegantly dressed in a blue Sambalpuri silk sari with silver borders, a hint of seductiveness and a faint smile on her face." He looked at Ajit, who seemed to be lost for the moment, transfixed to this almost royal entrance.

It must have been a few moments before Ajit came to his senses. He simply said, "Uncle, I am sorry, I was in a kind of fog. I was taken aback by that royal entrance," and with a dramatic voice, he added, "She is the Queen of Bhubaneswar."

For the moment, Ajit and Dr. Sonjee tried vainly to ignore the domineering royal presence and busied themselves in finishing the delectable South Indian dishes. After a few minutes, it was almost simultaneously that Ajit and Dr. Sonjee glanced at the Queen, who was presiding over her Court. There was an aura of excitement in the restaurant.

Ajit slowly resumed his introduction of the Queen. He said, "Uncle, she represents the Bhubaneswar constituency in the Parliament at New Delhi. She is not just a politician, she is the undisputed Queen of Bhubaneswar. She even claims she is a descendant of the Gajapati Royal family of Orissa. Politically, she is close to Prime Minister Indira Gandhi. You recall the Parliamentary elections in 1971. Just prior to it, the Prime Minister had sent the Indian Army to liberate Bangladesh from the clutches of the Pakistani military establishment. Her party won a thumping majority in Parliament. Yes, uncle, the Queen was elected to Parliament in that election."

Dr. Sonjee became impatient and interrupted Ajit, "What is so unique about it?" Again, Ajit took his time, glanced at the Queen and added, "She is a feminist. She is the leading voice for the women of India in Parliament. She even represented the women of India in the International Congress of Women in Mexico City."

Dr. Sonjee was still unimpressed. Ajit knew his uncle was getting impatient. He added, "I am simply trying to put myself together. It is not an easy story to tell." Ajit got up from his chair, agitated and anxious and with a quick look at the Queen, returned to his chair and resumed, "Actually, her real name is Sunanda. She was born in a small village near Bhubaneswar, raised in a middle-class family and graduated from the Womens' College of Bhubaneswar. Then, she was married around 1967."

Again, Ajit seemed preoccupied and almost with misty eyes, slowly said, "Uncle, she almost became a victim of murder, a statistic in the dowry deaths of Orissa. She was almost murdered by her husband and parents-in-law because she had not brought enough money and a scooter into the marriage."

Ajit had a far away look, misty eyed and Dr. Sonjee was stunned. He had left India many years back, knew that dowry deaths were on the increase in India and Orissa was no exception. Dr. Sonjee broke the silence and suggested, "I suppose the plot to murder her misfired. She divorced her husband and joined politics."

Ajit stated, "Uncle, your presumption is quite correct. She got out of the marriage, and joined the Congress Party of Indira Gandhi. She had this immense charisma and beauty. She can cast a spell over the audience. Mind you, the voters in India have common sense. They admire her for her dedication to the cause of women and for bringing them from the sixteenth to the twentieth century. If she were in America, I bet she would be in the Senate of your country."

Dr. Sonjee was still unimpressed. He asked Ajit, "How did she escape the murder?"

Ajit looked at the Queen and proceeded, "Sunanda's parents couldn't produce the money and other items promised as dowry at the time of the marriage. Sunanda was subjected to daily put-downs, tauntings, teasings and harassment, which gradually escalated to veiled threats. In this joint family, there were her husband, parents-in-law and Meena, a sixteen year old sister-in-law. Sunanda had known about young brides being burnt to death. She lived in terror. She managed to smuggle letters to her parents via Meena, informing them of the threats and the imminent danger she was facing."

Dr. Sonjee interjected, "I suppose, finally, she was able to escape from that oppressive and threatening situation with her parents' help."

Ajit responded, "Not quite, you know, running away from a husband does not happen in India. She resigned herself to fate."

Ajit remained silent for a while, again looked at the Queen still presiding over the group and engaged in animated discussion.

He proceeded, "I distinctly remember the day. It was June 10, 1968. It was a very hot summer day, an inferno. The monsoon had not yet broken. It was about eleven in the morning. I was in my office in Sahid Nagar. Suddenly, I was jolted from my office work with shoutings and wailings coming from the street nearby. Initially, I rejected the idea of getting up and investigating it. I thought it must be another of those countless street demonstrations which plague today's India, but there was something strange about this noise. There were no slogans as is usual with political demonstrations. It was like a mass wailing, like a thousand voices crying to the heavens. It was like the roar of the ocean. I came out and proceeded towards the crowd. It was not very far from the Hotel Meghdoot. As soon as I reached the crowd, I asked the first person what had happened. This man mumbled something like, 'They have burnt their daughter-in-law to death.' I proceeded with the jostling, milling crowd towards the house. There were intermittent threats from the crowd, 'Maro, Maro', that is, inciting the mob to kill the murderers of the innocent woman. Just a few feet from me, I saw my friend, Misra, a Police Officer, who was trying to control the crowd. I fought through the crowd, grabbed him by his hands and asked him anxiously about what had happened. Misra shook my hands and said, 'A female has died accidentally in the house fire, but the mob believes differently'. Misra charged furiously towards the house and I fell in back with the mob proceeding menacingly towards the house."

Dr. Sonjee interjected, "Was the mob on the verge of rioting? Was the mood like that in the Watts riots of Los Angeles in 1965 ?"

Ajit again looked at the Queen at the other corner of the restaurant listening to her followers, occasionally smiling. Just above her on the wall was a painting of the great Sun temple of Konarak.

Ajit finally responded, "No, uncle, the riots in Los Angeles were an acute culmination of the anger and despair of your African-Americans in that city. This mob, in contrast, was in a religious frenzy, a mass

hysteria, out to punish the murderers of the innocent bride. You know, the Goddess Kali descends to
the earth once a year to cleanse it of evils. The mob
began chanting to Goddess Kali in unison during
its menacing march towards that house. I became a
part of that crowd, which was now proceeding in
waves, occasionally shouting, 'Maro, Maro'. Finally,
the crowd reached the house. It had been surrounded
by hundreds of police. Smoke was coming out of
the house and it was barricaded. The crowd stopped,
continued to chant to Goddess Kali, but didn't try
to storm the barricades. Occasionally, threats were
shouted against the parents-in-law and the husband.
The crowd had made a judgment that it was a dowry
murder. It must have been an hour before a police
officer stood up on his jeep and made an announce-
ment that the charred body of a female had been
found and it was an accidental fire and not a dowry
murder. Then, he paused as if to calm the crowd
and added dramatically, "The body appeared to be
that of Meena and not the bride". The crowd was
stunned to silence, shocked because it had already
assumed that the bride was the victim of dowry
murder."

Dr. Sonjee interjected, "It was just an accidental
fire."

Ajit responded slowly, "Uncle, it is a confusing
story. My friend, Misra and the detectives had interrogated the parents-in-law and the husband of
the Queen. That evening I went to my friend's house
to get the facts. As far as I could piece it together
from what my friend told me, the accused burnt the
wrong victim, their own daughter, and sister. It

would appear that Meena didn't approve of the teasings, tauntings and threats from her parents and brother towards her sister-in-law. Remember, she was only sixteen, a very idealistic school girl. She had developed a close relationship with her sister-in-law, Sunanda. She kept her eyes and ears open. She overheard, with horror, the details of the diabolical plot outlined by her own mother to her father and brother late one night. Obviously, they had assumed that Meena was deep asleep in her room.

Let me put myself in her place for a moment. First, she might have thought it was a nightmare. Then, the plot unfolded and she heard it with bated breath. The day was set for the morning of June 10, 1968. The plot was crude, simple, grotesque and not unlike some Jewish victims thrown alive to the crematoria at the Auschwitz Nazi death camp in Poland during World War II. Obviously, Sunanda would be cooking in the kitchen and her parents-in-law and husband would surprise her in the kitchen. The men would suddenly jump on her like a tiger does to a deer, hold her tight and the mother-in-law would swiftly dowse her with kerosene and light a match, setting her on fire."

Dr. Sonjee interrupted Ajit, "Don't you think you are imagining too much, Ajit?" Ajit simply said, "Uncle, much of this has come from the confessions made by the guilty. Let me go on. On that fateful morning, Meena must have approached her sister-in-law to cook in her place. She must have cleverly arranged for Sunanda to get out of the house on some pretext. She must have borrowed her sister-in-law's sari and started the usual chores in the kitchen. She must have thought that as soon as her brother and father would overpower her, she would dramatically take off her sari from her face and confront them with their murderous intent. Obviously, she was a fraction of a second too late. You know, a murderer is so blinded with the act of crime that the victim becomes, for a moment, faceless. Now, you know what happened and how the Queen had cheated death."

Dr. Sonjee was stunned and speechless. When he got his senses back, he looked around. The restaurant was still full of people, bright lights, elegantly dressed diners, talking and laughing in that beautiful restaurant. Dr. Sonjee looked at the walls. With large paintings of the great temples of Orissa: Jagannath, Lingaraj and Konarak. Almost like a mechanical toy, he proceeded towards the table where the Queen was, to greet her, but the Queen and her entourage had departed.

He returned to his chair and asked Ajit, "What happened to Sunanda's husband and parents-in-law?" Ajit said, "They were found guilty of homicide and sentenced to life. They are now serving this sentence in the Central Jail at Cuttack."

Being a psychiatrist, Dr. Sonjee, of course, wanted to know how they were coping with this immense tragedy. Ajit said, "Uncle, occasionally, I follow thru with them via my contacts with officers in the jail. All three of them maintain that the dead body was that of Sunanda. They think the Queen is an impostor."

Dr. Sonjee asked, "How do they account for the fact that Meena is no more?"

Ajit became visibly agitated, almost holding his tears back. After he composed himself, he said, "They believe that Meena is in some ashram in Haradwar and that she has become a Sannyasin."

After a pause, Dr. Sonjee then asked about the mother-in-law who had apparently masterminded the entire plot. Ajit reported that she would frequently retire to a corner in her jail cell and wail, "Oh, Lord Jagannath, what crimes have I committed to deserve such harsh punishment ?"

As they were ready to leave, Dr. Sonjee put his arm around Ajit's shoulders and affectionately asked him, " Why are you so emotional about this story?"

Ajit laughingly responded, "Uncle, let me reserve that story for your next trip to Bhubaneswar."

THE WOMAN FROM AUSCHWITZ

T he mail came early this morning. The usual bills, payments, and ads were piled on my desk, but there was a letter in a light blue envelope that caught my eye. I decided to open it before seeing the patient who was waiting for me.

> 950 Olive Avenue
> Santa Cruz, CA 95060
> (408) 238-4276
> January 8, 1985

Dear Doctor Sonjee,

You will be most surprised to receive this letter. As you may recall we parted company some twenty-seven years ago in Little Rock, Arkansas. The memory of you had almost faded until just a few days ago when I had a bizarre flashback about you. I had no idea what triggered the memory of the summer of 1955 when we met at the University of Arkansas Hospital where I was an Occupational Therapist.

We were so different. I was a Jewish woman born in Hungary, who had survived the Nazi Death Camp, and you were a Hindu from India. Do you remember the hours we were together? There was chemistry between us. Was it love? I do not know. How can a Jewish woman fall in love with a superstitious Hindu, a devotee of Lord Jagannath? But I miss the days in Little Rock when you and I used to go to Tony's Pizzeria in the evenings and had so many long talks.

Why am I writing to you? I have had a desire for a long time to revisit Auschwitz but I do not want to go alone. When the thoughts of you came into my mind I knew I wanted you to go with me. We were such good friends and you were so sensitive and supportive of me in Little Rock when I would speak of my experiences. You may recall that my entire family was put to death at Auschwitz. It will be a difficult trip and of all the people I have known I feel deep inside that you are the person I would most like to be with.

My provisional plans are to go to Poland in mid-April, stay there for a month and perhaps visit my ancestral village in Hungary. Please call me right away.

Sincerely,
Sarah

I was shocked to read the letter. I was amazed that she remembered me after so many years and that she wanted me to go with her. I was distracted by the memories of Sarah as I prepared to see the

patient who was waiting for me. As I walked toward the room I recalled a vivacious young woman,
dark-haired, very beautiful and interested in Eastern philosophy. It was all I could do to get through
the session with my patient and get back to my desk
where I could read the letter again and contemplate
the request. It was an hour and a half later when I
finally had some free time to think about Sarah and
the years we knew each other.

I came to Little Rock in July of 1955. The capital
of Arkansas was a long, long way from the small
town in India where I had been living. I had done a
lot of reading about this wonderful country. I knew
I was going to the deep south and I was worried. In
those days the African-American citizens suffered
daily from discriminatory practices, insults, segregation in public transportation, parks and schools –
simply on the basis of skin color and their origin
from Africa as slaves. This great nation, almost
ninety years after Lincoln's Proclamation of Freedom, was still practicing dehumanization of her own
African-American citizens and violation of their
human rights. This was beyond my comprehension.
But I knew that Americans were hard working, honest, open and very patriotic. I had faith in the sense
of fairness of the American people. Nevertheless, I
was a bit apprehensive about my assignment in Arkansas as I am quite dark-skinned. I was fearful
of discrimination in public places. Should I continue
to identify myself as a person from India? Should I
keep a distance from African-Americans? Should I
protest and face the risk of being assaulted? Should
I just close my eyes to all this?

Luckily I had a reservation to stay in the hospital campus, an apartment complex for physicians in training. Thus, I reassured myself that I wouldn't have to look for an apartment or visit public eating places and be confronted with put-downs, dirty looks, or even denial of services. After collecting my luggage from the Greyhound bus, I hailed a taxi to take me to the hospital campus. The taxi driver, a big white man, gave me what I thought was a strange look. I told him of my destination and there was no conversation.

It was many months before I got used to the routine of hospital life and my work and training in the Department of Psychiatry at the University of Arkansas Medical Center. It was a bone-breaking routine. Psychiatry, in those days, was primarily psychotherapy-oriented and fully half of our time was devoted to doing psychotherapy with patients and having psychoanalysts supervise our work, as a learning mechanism. Actually, I was in the world of white people. Virtually all the psychiatrists in training were white. I felt no discrimination either from my white colleagues or from the nursing staff. I was quite well accepted. I suppose they made a distinction between a "black" Indian and their own black people. There were a few African-Americans in the low levels of employment in the hospital. Many psychiatric aides, the lowest in the nursing hierarchy, were African-Americans and I found them to be cheerful and very friendly. On the surface, things appeared to be very normal. Despite my comfort in the hospital setting I did not dare to go to public restaurants for fear of being insulted or even thrown out. Our Hindu mentality is to accept things without a fight. I decided that I would lead a low-key life and devote myself totally to training.

It was in the late winter of 1955-56 that I suffered from an episode of mental depression. I recall it was a combination of homesickness, loneliness, and a sense of isolation. I suffered from sleeplessness and poor appetite, lost weight and barely managed to do my job. I began to feel as if I might be in the wrong profession. During those dark days I somehow decided that I would ask Sarah, the Occupational Therapist, for a date. In our professional relationship we had numerous discussions about patient care and management and we got along very well. She was a warm, out-going person. I knew that she was a Jewish immigrant from Europe. Beyond that I didn't know anything about her. Of course she was a single woman. I debated for many days whether it would be appropriate to ask her for a date in this citadel of segregation and in the deep south of America. At times I visualized myself as being lynched in a public place for dating a white female in Little Rock. I also thought she might rebuff me on the basis of my skin color. It was a few more weeks before I had the courage to ask her for a date. To my utter surprise, she not only accepted but also seemed to be pleased.

Sarah and I went out frequently, mostly to movies or driving around the countryside and eating at restaurants close to the hospital campus. I genuinely liked her, an open and warm person with whom I felt very comfortable. Sometimes, she would invite me to her apartment for dinner. We would listen to music and talk about all kinds of things, mostly philosophical issues, about life and death and destiny, and about religions. Did we fall in love? I don't know. It was friendship, but complicated because I was a male and she was a female. We became close. To be with each other became natural to us. She knew I was a Hindu from Orissa, the Land of Jagannath in India and I knew she was Jewish, having come to America as a girl after World War II.

As I recall it was many months of friendship before the following story emerged. After a very hectic week at the hospital we decided to visit several places around Little Rock on a fabulous Saturday. I think it was the summer of 1956. We decided to go on a picnic to the Washington Park on Lake Maumelle some 25 miles down Hwy 10. Sarah insisted that I make an Indian dish, which I did. It probably was an awful chicken curry. In that beautiful park we ate our picnic lunch and then went on a long walk. Then we sat under an ancient oak tree and I was almost ready to take a nap. We were both absorbed in our own thoughts. I was drifting off to sleep when I heard sobbing, a soft sobbing full of sorrow but not wailing or hysteria. I opened my eyes and noticed that Sarah was not around. I looked around among the people in the park and spotted her by the side of the water. She was perhaps about forty feet from me. I looked at her closely and realized she was the one who was sobbing. I did not know what to do. Should I go and find out or just leave her alone? It was several minutes before I went over to her. She made no eye contact with me. Again not knowing what to do I sat near her waiting and then held her hand in a tight squeeze. It was several minutes before Sarah stopped sobbing. She simply said, "I am sorry." I again waited, put my arms around her and drew her close to my chest. She didn't resist and after what appeared to be a long silence she said, "I am sorry. I am re-living some old trauma. You know it was eleven years ago to this date that I was liberated from Auschwitz by Russian soldiers."

For a moment Auschwitz did not register with me and then all of a sudden it struck me like a blow on my head with shock and disbelief. I almost lost control and shouted, "Sarah, do you mean the Nazi death camp at Auschwitz-Birkenau in Poland? Are you sure you are not making it up or daydreaming about something in war-torn Europe? Sarah, are you sure of what you just told me?"

Sarah, who was in my arms, looked at me with a faint but sad smile, "Yes, I was a prisoner at Auschwitz. I was sent there along with my parents, brother and sister from Hungary in the early spring of 1944. I was about fifteen then." I could hardly believe that this woman in my arms was a survivor of the Nazi death camp. Sarah was looking at the high heavens and again, started sobbing. I knew she was crying her heart out. I imagined those cries were still reverberating a thousand times in the now abandoned Auschwitz. Finally she stopped crying and said, "I do not know why I am telling you all this." Then she started laughing and added, "You know, I don't need any psychiatric treatment."

I did not know what to say. I let her lie on my chest. Then she said, "Eleven years ago today I became a free woman, no, a girl mind you, age 16." Again, there was a long pause. It was just beginning to sink into me that this woman had gone through a living hell and survived. There was no parallel in all of human history like the Nazi death camps. I was aroused from my nightmarish thoughts with a shocking statement and it was, "My parents, brother and sister didn't survive. They were gassed in the death chambers and their bodies consigned to the crematory." All I could say was, "Oh my God, Oh my God." I held Sarah close to my chest and gave her a kiss on her cheek. She squeezed my hand affectionately.

Yes, I had read about the Nazi death camps, but to be confronted with it by a survivor was beyond my tolerance. I was no longer at that moment a doctor training to be a psychiatrist in Little Rock. I said to her, "Sarah will you please join me in a prayer to our Lord Jagannath?" She sat up. We knelt, held hands and I prayed aloud, "Oh Jagannath, you claim to be the Lord of the Universe and God of all people on this earth, regardless of religion. And you let this happen to innocent Jewish people, and you let them die. Didn't you hear the cries of those Jewish prisoners from the death camps of Poland and Germany? You Black God, you failed in your duties to the Jewish people. You ought to be ashamed of yourself. You God of all peoples... " At this point I couldn't go on and started crying. Sarah held me to her bosom. We both lay there speechless.

My relationship with Sarah continued on a platonic basis for another two years. We talked frequently, intensively and extensively about her experiences at Auschwitz, her life in Hungary, the Jewish traditions and festivals of a bygone era. I talked about the Jagannath, the temples of Orissa, the history of three great religions, Buddhism, Jainism and Hinduism, which profoundly influenced Orissa and the terrors inflicted on the people of Orissa by the Muslim invaders. We remained close with much mutual affection and respect. Was I in love with her? Perhaps, but I am not sure. Was she in love with me? Who knows?

It was about 1958 that I completed my training in Little Rock and decided to relocate in Toledo, Ohio to start a private practice in Psychiatry. Sarah continued at the University of Arkansas Medical Center. Finally we parted in sadness. We knew this was no ordinary friendship between us and that we would treasure the memories of each other until we died.

I immersed myself in setting up practice in Toledo. Time is a great healer. I made new friends and life went on. I got married, had one child. With all the stresses and strains of being a psychiatrist, life was relatively stable and predictable.

Then this letter from Sarah came, almost 27 years after we had parted company. This was no ordinary letter. I could not keep it out of my mind. I became obsessed with it. At times I thought someone might be playing a trick on me. Should I call her to verify? Should I just throw this letter away? Should I consult with Dr. Rosenberg? As a child he had escaped the horrors of Nazi Germany, having migrated with his family to Cincinnati. Something inside me told me that I should make the call myself, not on anyone's advice. Why should I, a busy psychiatrist, disrupt my life and practice, leave my family and go on this wild trip to Auschwitz? After all, I said to myself, it was now all history. Some people do not even believe that the Holocaust happened, that it is a figment of the imagination of some Jewish people. Furthermore, why should I, a Hindu doctor in America, be so concerned with Holocaust and Nazism, death camps of Hitler and this Jewish female survivor? I am not even a Jew. I do not know much about Judaism. Why should I be sucked into this wild trip to Auschwitz with a woman I knew so long ago? Regardless of how much I tried to distance myself from Sarah's request I just couldn't shake it off. Perhaps, it was an invitation from Yama, the God of Death in our Hindu Pantheon. I have always been fascinated with Death. Sarah has been near death, not a natural death, but near being murdered just because she was a Jewish girl in Hungary. I was tempted to make this trip to the unknown. I was having nightmares, strangely not about death and dying, but about happenings of my own childhood, such as the loss of a brother when I was three years old. I tried hard to search my soul. Why should I be tempted to make this trip and in search of what? It was such a bizarre proposal, a Hindu psychiatrist and a Jewish survivor of Auschwitz making a trip to Poland after forty years of being liberated from that death camp. Days went by and I remained obsessed with it.

One foggy morning I was walking in Jefferson Park near the lake in Toledo. As usual, I was preoccupied with that letter from Sarah. It dawned on me that of all the human tragedies in human history, the Holocaust stands out as something beyond comprehension. Sure we Hindus in India were persecuted by Muslim invaders who destroyed some of our beautiful temples. Still we Hindus have remained accepting of others. I pondered over a panoramic view of history of India since pre-historic times. I could find no parallel in this history to Auschwitz and the Holocaust. I decided I must go to Auschwitz with Sarah, even though I did not know what might happen to either of us. That same evening I called Sarah at Santa Cruz. I told her I would accompany her to Auschwitz. Her crisp response was, "I had no doubt that you would."

We were to meet at JFK Airport on April 13 and take a flight to Krakow, Poland via Frankfurt, Germany. We were to meet at the Lufthansa Airlines flight 75 boarding area about two hours before the departure. I was there on time and looked around for Sarah. A number of passengers were already in the boarding area. I had the fear that I wouldn't recognize her. I glanced around, casting furtive glances at all the women, and became convinced Sarah was not there. I had a momentary feeling that all this was a big hoax.

I was getting nervous. Suddenly as if from nowhere a woman appeared and gave me a hug and a kiss on my lips. She held me tight. She didn't say anything. I had closed my eyes and found myself softly saying, "Sarah, Sarah". Obviously both of us were oblivious to our surroundings for a few moments. Finally she let me go and held my hands, then we sat down, and we made eye contact. I found her still extraordinarily beautiful despite the passage of twenty-seven years. She radiated warmth. She was calm in contrast to my own inner agitation and confusion. I was speechless. She held my hand tightly, gently caressing it. For a moment I thought she was behaving like a wife. I was aware of the old sexual feelings toward her that were rising like storms within me. Attempting to suppress my feelings, I asked Sarah about her flight from California. She probably sensed what was happening to me as she let go of my hand and we engaged in a routine conversation. We talked about our mutual friends and our days in Little Rock as we waited to board our flight. We didn't discuss the bizarre trip we were about to take.

It was a smooth, long flight to Frankfurt and on to Krakow, Poland. During that time I was vaguely aware of an unpredictable, unknown situation and a sense of anxiety. Our conversations were similar to those we had in Little Rock. As usual, she was verbal, animated, spontaneous and charming. By contrast I was stilted, at times evasive, and not so charming. I had always wondered why she was attracted to me. Though we didn't talk about our mission I knew something was going to happen.

It was evening when we arrived at the Krakow airport. Surprisingly it was a very busy airport. Sarah observed the crowds and made the remark that perhaps Jewish survivors or sons and daughters of those who had perished at Auschwitz-Birkenau were making the same trips that we were. She had made a reservation at a small hotel for us at Oswiecim, a small town nearby. We checked into our rooms and had dinner. During dinner, Sarah made no mention of the mission. When we each retired to our rooms she simply stated that the next morning after breakfast we were to take a bus to Auschwitz. She said this in such a matter-of-fact way that it was almost unreal. I reflected on the fact that so many people had arrived here on cattle trains from Nazi-dominated Europe in the cruel illusion of coming to a rehabilitation camp. Only the Nazis could invent such a euphemism.

I had a restless night. What was I doing here in Poland? I thought I must have been insane to undertake this trip. My mind went back to a secure and predictable childhood in India. I got comfort from such memories. This Holocaust was beyond my comprehension.

It was a beautiful morning. I met Sarah in the dining room of the hotel. I asked her how she slept and her cheery response was "Fine." She asked, "How about you?" I told her that I had a restless night. She smiled. We had a good breakfast. I was rather stunned that Sarah was behaving like a tourist, no real emotions, no complaints so far about the Nazis, no tears.

We took a bus along with a number of others on our way to Auschwitz-Birkeanu. There was an almost eerie silence on the bus. Obviously, some had come from Israel, some from America and from other lands. Finally we arrived at the camp.

There were already a number of buses with hundreds of people of all ages entering the campsite. Sarah and I followed the crowd. We noticed that there was some kind of ceremony going on. We

quickened our paces towards that area. We saw rab-
bis with richly embroidered prayer shawls walking
along. I felt a little out of place in a Jewish ceremony
in memory of those who were gassed, starved,
clubbed, hung, shot and finally consigned to the cre-
matorium.

The ceremony started. The Israeli cantor's prayer
with unbridled anger recalled those whose ashes still
lingered in the fields and ponds forty years after
Soviet soldiers liberated Auschwitz. This ceremony
was being conducted in the world's biggest graveyard. Sarah and I were holding hands. Her grip on
my hand was tightening but she was in rapt attention to the speakers. Anyone could come and speak
for a minute or two. A man in a wheelchair, obviously in his eighties, came up to speak. His voice
was trembling, "I still have the same fear now as I
had walking on these grounds forty years ago. I still
see the faces of those who are not here. I still see the
SS guards. Sometimes I imagine one of them coming towards me with a bayonet and I scream. I fight
him back with bare hands. Over there under that
tree a young Jewish girl would regularly pass by me
and hand over a piece of dry bread. She was working in the kitchen. On the other side of that building Aaron, my friend, fought a Nazi guard with bare
hands. He was shot repeatedly by two Nazis.
Despite those bullet holes in his body he kept trying to stand up and go after one of them. Finally he
laid on the feet of a Nazi who kicked the dead body
like a maniac until he himself collapsed. I thought
to myself as long as there are Jews like Aaron, Judaism will survive." Sarah still showed no emotion

but suddenly I felt a jerk on my hand and she started pulling me towards the platform. Obviously she was going to speak. I resisted going with her but she seemed to be so strong. For a moment I thought I would simply pass out. She whispered a reassuring word into my ear, "Come on. I will speak a few words and you can speak if you wish." I thought I was participating in a most bizarre phenomenon. Nevertheless, I went along, quite self-conscious but with full realization that Sarah had this in mind when she had invited me to come along with her.

We went up holding hands. She spoke very briefly, "Today I come here with no thoughts of Holocaust, of Nazism, of SS Guards, of gas chambers and crematory. I am here today to call on my parents, brother and sister from Heaven to listen to me." At that moment, Sarah stretched her hands towards the sky and said, "Mama, Papa, Moritz and Helene, do you hear me? I am here today at Auschwitz. Deep, deep in my heart, there is a place where I talk with you every day. I do not talk to you about Auschwitz. I talk to you about our village in Hungary, our good days together, and as long as I am alive I will talk with you daily. You will live within me." At that point Sarah gave me a hug, threw a kiss towards the audience and introduced me. She said, "This is Dr. Sonjee, a Hindu friend of mine. The Hindus believe in re-incarnation and I asked him to say a few words." With that Sarah nudged me towards the microphone. I have never been a good speaker. What could I say in this strange and historic place where 1.5 million Jews were murdered? I took a deep breath. I was certainly not prepared for this. I looked up towards the heavens and said, "Oh Jagannath, the God of all peoples of the world, didn't you hear the cries of millions of Jewish men, women and children as they were being murdered in Europe? Did you remain blind to their sufferings because they were non-Hindu? Haven't you claimed again and again that the entire Universe lies within you? Let my message to you reverberate within your great Temple at Puri and let there be, from now on, deep friendship and love between the Hindus and the Jews." With that I wiped my tears away and came away from the platform.

The ceremony continued for another hour or so. Sarah and I, along with many others, cried much of the time. At the end Sarah looked for the man in the wheelchair and I followed her. We found him surrounded by family and friends. Sarah found her way through them and stood in front of him. She bent down and gave him a kiss and hug and gently said, "Simon, I'm sorry I do not have your piece of bread today." There was a stunning silence for a moment. I have inadequate words to describe the scene that followed. Sarah was literally mobbed by the crowd around the man. There were tears of joy. Someone started singing a Jewish folksong from Hungary and people started dancing around Sarah. I was lost in the crowd. I realized that I was witnessing a beautiful story of love in a place filled with so many memories of hate and death. This was happiness and love the Nazis couldn't eliminate.

We next visited the nearby museum where there were remnants and relics of Auschwitz, including human hair. Each item was a reminder of an event or a story of indescribable suffering. I became numb and I told Sarah that I could not take any more. I was surprised at her seeming composure. Many people greeted me and Sarah. One little girl about 10 years old stopped us. She said, "I am Freida. I am from Tel Aviv. Over there are my parents. I would like to ask you something. My grandparents died at this camp. You said you believe in re-incarnation. Does it mean that my grandparents have been reborn, and if so, where are they and how can I find them?" I kneeled down and held her hands. I said, "We Hindus believe in re-incarnation. We believe that the body dies but the soul never does. It enters another body. About your grandparents, I do not know where they are. When you grow up I hope you can go to India and experience the faith and devotion of the Hindus. I know you feel there are many things that do not seem to make sense, but my faith shows me they ultimately do."

Sarah and I made the final trip to the gas chambers and the crematoria, stark witnesses to one of the most horrible examples of man's inhumanity to man. Only at this point Sarah sobbed just as she had in the park near Little Rock. I couldn't come up with any words to console her. I held Sarah to my chest and wept silently. Many people around us were also crying.

We returned to the hotel. Neither one of us was in any conversational mood. We had no desire to stay any more in Poland. The next day we took a flight out of Krakow and returned to New York. As we walked through JFK airport, I was in a partial daze but Sarah was recovering rather rapidly. I wondered how she could be so cheerful considering that she had just returned from the site where she had been near death for more than a year. She was quite chatty and began to console me. She kept talking about her childhood in Hungary. The memories and images were sharp and not unlike mine from my small town in India. Finally we sat in a lounge to wait, as we had many hours before our respective flights, hers to California and mine to Chicago. Finally I thought I might now ask her the question as to why she had asked me, of all the people she knew, to come with her to Auschwitz. She was for a moment taken aback at this question. Obviously she was not expecting it. For a moment she seemed agitated and then she started laughing. She was becoming quite loud. She caught the attention of others in the lounge. I was feeling embarrassed. She sat closer to me and gave me a gentle kiss and said, "Didn't you realize that I was in love with you in Little Rock? I am still in love with you. I know you are married now." Then she laughed and said, "Maybe in our next lives."

I was stunned and confused. I had the urge to run away. I flashed back to our friendship in Little Rock. I knew the relationship was more than platonic but I never could make the next move. I kissed Sarah and said, "Sarah, we Hindus also believe in destiny. I guess that it was not to be." We hugged each other as a final good-bye.

Her flight was being announced and I accompanied her to the boarding area, kissed her again, and said, "Maybe in our next lives." She laughed and wiped away a tear and we parted.

It has been almost six years since my trip to Auschwitz. It was difficult for me to forget the experience and get into my routine, but time is a great healer and I found my life took on a new dimension after that. I was also able to look at the entire panorama of the history of the Jewish people from a different perspective. I realized that the ups and downs of the Jewish people parallel other cultures and groups, but the Holocaust surpassed all tragedies of human history. I say that I too have ups and downs, but nothing I can't handle or learn from, and I saw how life goes on.

Sarah and I didn't contact each other for years but in the early part of 1991 I was surprised to receive a letter postmarked Puri. I had not been corresponding with anyone in Puri. I opened the letter and read it, and re-read it.

Puri, Orissa, India
January 21, 1991

Dear Dr. Sonjee:

I am sure you are surprised to receive this letter from me. I am in Puri and have been here for almost two years. After our trip to Auschwitz my life changed. I was no longer interested in the material, mundane aspects of my life. I continued in my profession for awhile but all along I felt powerful urges to do something different. I studied your Hindu scriptures and the Bhagavad Gita. I became a regular attendant in discourses in Hindu philosophy as given by various Swamis visiting the area. Having no family of my own it was not that difficult to make the final decision. I became a Sannyasin and decided to move to Puri as a devotee of Jagannath. Here I have started a training center for women who have no home, and helping them toward self-sufficiency has been very rewarding. I have learned to speak Oriya. I visit the Jagannath temple daily. Since I am of non-Hindu origin I am not allowed to enter the temple, but I pray from outside the Lion Gate. You remember the beautiful pillar from the Konarak Temple in front of the gate? I stand near the pillar and pray to Jagannath. I am now at peace with my life. The nightmare of Auschwitz is no longer with me. The work I am doing with these women is immensely gratifying. My training center has your father's name, 'Mrutyunjaya' meaning Conqueror of Death. Perhaps you do not remember your telling me about your father. The training center is very close to the Chaitanya Ashram. I would like you to visit me here on you next trip to Puri.

You may be wondering what it was that inspired me to be a devotee of Lord Jagannath and start this project in Puri. Well, it was your friendship. As I wrote you in my first letter in 1985 we are of very different backgrounds, I am a Jewish woman born in Hungary who had survived the Nazi Death Camp, and you are a Hindu from India. Do you remember the hours we were together? There was chemistry between us. Was it love? I don't know. How could I fall in love with a superstitious Hindu, a devotee of Lord Jagannath? I have to admit now that I have been in love with you ever since our days at Little Rock. Even though it is the love of a woman for a man it transcends religions, backgrounds and countries. Yes, my love for you is intense and will remain so. Perhaps in our next lives we will be together.

Love, Sarah

That evening I went to my favorite park near Lake Erie in Toledo. It was getting dark and very cold. The park was quiet and silent. I happened to be the only person under this huge tree. I let myself go. I outstretched my hands towards the sky and looked east towards India and yelled at the top of my voice, "Sarah, Sarah, you have shown the world that the suffering you and your people endured can be transformed into great love and beautiful service. Bless you, Sarah. You have defeated the Nazis again!" With that I threw a kiss towards her in a distant land.

TRAIN TO HARDWAR

In the summer of 1977, south Florida was experiencing abnormally hot weather. I had a busy psychiatric practice in Sarasota. Additionally, I had the responsibility for the psychiatric treatment of the mentally ill prisoners in the local jail. One of these patients, a forty year old male, had committed suicide. Another patient, a female of twenty-six and mother of two small children, had managed to escape and her whereabouts, even after ten days of her disappearance, were unknown. Both of these patients were under my care. Perhaps, I was suffering from burn-out. Having come from a poverty-stricken background in India, I had this immense hunger for success and the need to be recognized as a good psychiatrist. I was depressed. I knew I was not functioning too well in my work. I had a few sessions of therapy and counseling. The outcome of these sessions was a recommendation by my therapist that I should go on a vacation to India.

In November of that year I left for India. My trips to India usually consist of family visits, friends, trips to museums and places of my growing-up in Orissa. I needed to revisit those places and sights, and to remember my friends who have passed away. Of course, I very much enjoyed the culture of Orissa. My trip to Orissa was coming to an end. I was spending my last week in Sambalpur, where I grew up. As I recall it was around nine in the evening; I was getting ready to retire in my room in the Tribeni Hotel, when there was a knock on the door. I had had a very busy day and I was a bit annoyed at this late call, but I realized that I was in India. I opened the door for a middle-aged male probably in his fifties, who had his hands folded and said, "Namaskar." I returned his greetings, but failed to recognize him. I said, "Please come in but I am sorry, I don't recall you." The stranger laughed and said, "Dr. Sonjee, it has been almost thirty years since I saw you. I am Krishna, you recall. I was about a year junior to you in high school." In a flash, I recognized him, a serious student, a philosopher of a kind, a non-conformist who liked to argue and who was in our school days, a close friend of mine. I hugged him and I was then speechless. I could only say, "I am very glad to see you again after so many years." There was a moment of discomfort and tension. He was quiet. I asked him if I could help. Krishna stood up, paced in the room and proceeded to tell me the following:

"Dr. Sonjee, I am sorry to intrude on your time and vacation. Please forgive me. I have been ruminating whether to come and talk with you or not. Only this evening, I decided I should. You know, we make friends or enemies in our life. Most of the friends pass from memory but some do not. In my case, you are one of my friends who lives within me. You remember, we spent many hours together walking after school. After high school, we parted company. Perhaps, you do not realize that I felt deeply when I knew that you had decided to stay in America. I thought, here was another of my dear friends who deserted his own country, who became untrue to Mother India, who became seduced by the Almighty Dollar and forgot his people."

I was getting a bit defensive and angry at this lecture and said, "Krishna, I am tired. Please come to the point. I do not wish to argue with you about my staying in America."

Krishna smiled and said, "You Americans are so impatient. Let me resume. You see, my pain at the fact of your staying in America was due to my long friendship with you. I thought, a precious phase of my life, that is, my friendship with you, was going to die. However, I was wrong. If it had died, I wouldn't be here today."

Krishna proceeded, "Just before you departed for America, I had joined the Orissa Police service. Currently, I am the Superintendent of Police of Bolangir District." At this point, Krishna got up from the chair and complained that he was getting light-headed. I offered him a glass of water. He seemed to feel better and he resumed, "You see, my wife passed away two years ago. My only daughter, Sunanda, is happily married. I am doing well in my job. Though I am 51, I have no desire to get remarried."

Then, he exploded with laughter and stated, "I am too old to get remarried, though I have had offers".

I was getting impatient at this long-winded story. I couldn't control myself. "It is getting late. Please come to the point." I didn't think this produced any effect. He took his time. He proceeded, "Dr. Sonjee, you know our Hindu concept of Vanaprastha, being an ascetic. I am thinking of severing all my attachments and departing permanently for Hardwar, to go there and to meditate about life. As you are a psychiatrist, I thought, I would come and consult with you." I asked him incredulously, "Do you mean that you will give up your job, family, friends, relatives and depart permanently to the Himalayas to be an ascetic with no assets, no income and to be resigned to the life of a beggar?" He simply said, "Precisely so. I have meditated about this for many years. I have studied all our Hindu scriptures. Do you have an opinion on my plan? This is why I am here today."

I asked myself, should I care? Here is an old friend of mine who wants to be totally detached and pursue knowledge in the holy city of Hardwar. I haven't seen him in many, many years. Let him go. However, there was something else. During my long walks in my hometown in America, I myself would sometimes daydream about Vanaprastha. After all, life was not that easy in Sarasota. I became curious.

I asked, "Krishna, you said you have studied the scriptures of Hinduism. As I understand it, Vanaprastha, literally means a 'forest dweller', that is, withdrawal and finally, to make oneself a hermit in the forests near a village. You might be referring to being a Sannyasi, a wandering Holy Man, when you talk about going to Hardwar. Why Hardwar? Why not go to Bodh Gaya where the great Buddha received Enlightenment? Why not go to Saranath, where He gave his first sermon?" I was getting carried away with my fantasies of being a Holy Man. Krishna was all attention.

After a pause, he said, "Dr. Sonjee, why Hardwar I am not sure, but I will come to that later on. Am I going astray? Am I thinking of Vanaprastha as a way of escape? Am I reacting to the loss of a very loving and devoted wife? Do I have some deep psychological problem? You see, I am confused. There is something in me emerging that tells me to do it. As a psychiatrist, you might have an understanding of what I am going through."

I said,"You remember, our festivals of Sambalpur, specifically the car festival and the festival of new rice and the memorable Sital Sasthi, the marriage ceremony of Shiva and Parvati. I too day-dream of being a wandering Holy Man in India even if I am a psychiatrist in America. However, I do not have the courage and the motivation to take such a leap. No, I do not think you are confused. You are following the tradition of our forefathers of several centuries back. But are you sure in your mind that you are emotionally ready to be detached?"

Krishna walked to the window, looked down on that empty street outside. It was close to midnight. He sat down on his chair and said, "It has not been an easy decision. It is a step into the unknown. After all, life is transitory."

Krishna got up and said good-bye. I held his hands and wished him good luck. I walked out to the street with him. It was quiet, past mid-night. There was hardly any activity. Krishna said he was just going to walk home and that it was no more than a mile. I asked him which day he was leaving for Hardwar. He simply said, "Day after tomorrow." I felt a sadness, something difficult to describe, also an admiration for a childhood friend who was walking into the unknown in search of truth and wisdom in the foothills of the Himalayas. Also I had a touch of envy.

I turned up at the Sambalpur train station to say a final good-bye to Krishna. Surprisingly, there was an immense crowd assembled in the train station. My nephew who had accompanied me made way for us through the crowd. I heard people shouting in unison, "Swami Krishna Ki Jai", meaning victory to Swami Krishna. Krishna had not arrived. The vast crowd was waiting for him patiently. I heard some music and a band playing an old Indian movie song. I looked over my shoulder and saw a jeep with a half-dozen people and Krishna standing, in a saffron robe with hands folded, smiling and greeting people. The jeep was moving slowly. The procession ended and Krishna was accompanied by a number of people to the platform. There was a decorated stage and he was escorted there to make a speech.

Krishna stood and, with folded hands, addressed the crowd. He said, "A few months after my wife died, I had a dream in which Lord Shiva was calling me to take this step to go to Hardwar where our

Mother Ganges touches the plains. I will meditate and be an ascetic. I am being reborn to lead a new life. This train journey will take me to Hardwar and beyond that, I do not know."

The crowd again shouted, "Long Live Swamiji." The whistle blew and the train was ready to start. At that point, he looked at me in the crowd and came running and held my hands. We exchanged no words, two friends, one shortly returning to a comfortable life in America and the other going to be a hermit.

A few days later, I returned to America. Gradually, the episode faded. I knew that it was not rare, even for well-placed Hindus to follow the path of my friend, Krishna.

It was around Christmas of 1994 that an international meeting for psychiatrists was being held in Delhi. Certainly, December is a pleasant time of the year in Sarasota, Florida, but I decided to attend this meeting and experience the culture and enjoy the sounds and sights of Delhi. It began to dawn on me that I might even pay a visit to Hardwar to see Krishna. I thought, he must have returned home within a matter of days after the initial spell of Hardwar had faded away. I recalled that one of his brothers was still in Sambalpur and I decided to write to him, to locate any particular address of Krishna at Hardwar. Amazingly, I received a prompt response from his brother, who wrote that he was living in a hermitage in Mayapur, a small town south of Hardwar. Beyond that, he didn't give any specifics.

I decided that I would go and look for Krishna

and learn from him about his search for wisdom and truth. I visualized Krishna as a Holy Man immersed in meditation on the bank of the Ganges or in some of the abandoned temples. I had this sense of vicarious fantasy that it was not Krishna but I was the Holy Man wandering around Hardwar, totally devoid of any attachments and desires.

At the end of my stay in Delhi, I made plans to take a trip to Hardwar. I took an early morning bus and was at Hardwar around four that afternoon. I checked into a hotel and decided to search for Krishna next morning.

I was up early and determined, like any Hindu, to first visit the Hari-ka-charan bathing ghat where the footmark of Vishnu is imprinted on a stone slab in the upper wall of the ghat. Here was one of the most sacred spots of pilgrimage for Hindus and it was a sublime experience to visit this spot as many of my forefathers had done.

I was there early in the morning and visited the ghat and the nearby temple and the entrance of the Ganges. There were many devotees even at the early hours of the morning and I was experiencing something that I had always wished to do.

I took a taxi to Mayapur and asked the driver if he knew of any nearby hermitages. He took me to the main market in Mayapur and pointed towards the foothills. Left alone I could see in the distance ruined buildings and temples. A crowd gathered around me. Many volunteered to help me with a small amount of reward. I asked one of the older men if he knew of anyone from Orissa. He didn't know such a person but volunteered to accompany me. I had selected him because he could speak English well. He told me that he was a graduate with a major in History and that he was eking out a living by helping foreign tourists. We walked up the trail to the foothills. Occasionally, there were ruined and abandoned temples, and Buddhist monasteries. My guide, Raghuvir, informed me that Hsuan Tsang, the Chinese Buddhist pilgrim had visited this area in the 7th century. I was struck by the great natural beauty of the area, with temples and hills and the the Ganges below. On the trail to our left were the ruins of an old fort. Raghuvir couldn't throw any light on the history of it. However, he gave me a good background on the history of Hardwar and descriptions of the Kumbh Festival held here every 12th year.

We stopped at a snack shop on the trail to rest, eat, and ask people about Krishna. Raghuvir was well known to the people there. He questioned them about someone coming from Orissa some 17 years back. They conversed in Hindi and Raghuvir was nice enough to translate it to me. I began to think that I was out of my mind, looking for a long lost friend in or near Hardwar after some 17 years but for a brief encounter with him at Sambalpur. Here I was a psychiatrist in Florida on a mysterious adventure. I was in a prayerful mood surrounded by places so sacred to Hindus. I had always wondered in America if I was a Hindu only on the surface, a fake with no real convictions. At this point, I was interrupted by Raghuvir, who said, "Dr. Sonjee, Lord Shiva will help you in this search. My friends here tell me that an Oriya came here many, many years back. They did not know his name. They thought that he lived in one of the Buddhist ruins, about five kilometers away."

We proceeded on a trail and ascended the hills. I had a beautiful view of the Ganges coming down to the plains near Hardwar.

It must have been close to evening when we arrived at the ruins. On the right side of the trail about forty feet below, there appeared to be a statue of Buddha. I wished to go down to look at it but Raghuvir warned me not to go down the trail. We were still going up. In the distance, I saw several caves or ruins, perhaps temples. There was no evidence of human activity. I was not sure that any human beings would be able to survive around here. Raghuvir, always encouraging, said, "We will find your friend."

The sun was setting and the sky was a myriad of colors. I could see the Ganges below. Finally, we were descending into a valley. I saw more ruins and, in the distance, I saw some people. There were many more ruins. I saw caves carved out of the rocks. We were now quite close to those ruins. My heart pounded. I was getting anxious. Raghuvir seemed to feel it and said reassuringly, "We will find your friend, Krishna." I was amazed at the optimism of the people of India. I knew that having been in America for so many years, I had lost that sense. Finally, I thought we were close to the ruins, caves and hills carved out of gigantic rocks.

I was getting impatient when suddenly a person in saffron robes came out of one of the caves.

Raghuvir quickly approached him and asked him in Hindi, "Sir, Dr. Sonjee here has come from America to find a friend from Orissa who might be around here. He came in 1977. His friend's name is Krishna." The man burst into a laugh and said, "You mean, this Dr. Sonjee is looking for a friend who left for the Himalayas in 1977." At this point, I introduced myself thus, "I am a psychiatrist in America. My friend, Krishna, came to see me in 1977 in Orissa before he left for Vanaprastha at Hardwar. I happened to be in Delhi and I wanted to look him up." At this he laughed again and said, "How can you be a psychiatrist? You are a bit crazy yourself, looking for a friend after 17 years in the foothills near Hardwar? It is like looking for a needle in a haystack." At this remark, I laughed and said, "You are right. I am a bit crazy. You see, I myself had wanted to be a Holy Man. At least, I have had such fantasies of being a hermit at Hardwar. That is why I am here. I want to find out how my friend, Krishna, has been doing and what knowledge and wisdom he has gained." The man in the saffron robe smiled sweetly and said, "I do not think anyone from Orissa lives around here. I have heard that a former police officer from Orissa lives in an abandoned Buddhist temple with caves around it. I wish you luck." With that, he came over, shook my hands, laughed, and said, "This is a crazy world."

Raghuvir and I followed his vague directions on a trail. The scene was wildly beautiful. It was getting dark. We arrived at a cluster of ruins and there were some lamps. Finally, we were approaching a cave and saw a man in saffron robes in a dimly lit cave. Raghuvir again gave the purpose of my visit and asked him if anyone by the name of Krishna was living around here. The man burst out laughing and shook his head and said, "Your friend Krishna lives in a cave way over there. He is a friend of mine. You see, I too was a high ranking Police Officer in Madras and I came here around 1982."

I couldn't help but ask him, "Have you found Wisdom and Truth? Are you enlightened?"

He laughed and simply said, "You ask Krishna those questions."

Raghuvir and I followed the directions and soon, we were at the cave. Just after we arrived at the cave, I saw a man darting from inside the cave with a big smile and outstretched hands coming towards me, with words, "Dr. Sonjee, I was expecting you. I knew one of these days, you would come. When we said good-bye at the Sambalpur train station some 17 years back, I had the feeling that I was going on to Vanaprastha but that it could have been you." He invited both of us inside the cave lit only with a kerosene lantern. He had us sit down on a mat. He invited us to stay overnight as his guests.

Raghuvir remained silent throughout our conversation. We talked about our old boyhood days in Sambalpur. Both of us were very very happy to see each other. I assumed that I would stay here for at least three days before I would return to Delhi to catch my flight to New York. It was wonderful to be with a Holy Man in a cave near Hardwar and specifically, that the Holy Man being a boyhood friend. I noticed that the cave was not quite enclosed and there was an opening on the back wall. Perhaps, the entire cave was about fifty square feet. There were blankets piled up on the floor. Luckily, I had brought a sort of overnight bag with me.

There was a lull in the conversation and Krishna announced that dinner would be served soon. At that point, he rang a bell. A person emerged from the back opening. For a moment, I had difficulty in seeing the person clearly. It was so dim. Suddenly, light shone on the face and chest and what I saw struck me like lightning. It was a very beautiful young woman, probably in her late thirties, of perhaps Chinese or Japanese origin. I was thunderstruck. I looked at Krishna as if imploring him to enlighten me on this presence. Krishna's face was inscrutable. I looked at Raghuvir as if he could tell me something about this lady. After what appeared to be a long interval, Krishna broke into a smile and said, "Let me introduce to you my wife, Akiko. She is from Kyoto, Japan. She came here about 10 years back to meditate. She is a devout Buddhist."

I was speechless. I looked at her fine features. She stood there like a statue, very beautiful,with cropped hair, and a saffron robe. I looked at my friend, Krishna, who had that enigmatic smile. It was too much for me.

Finally, I was able to mutter, "Krishna, you are married to her? You mean, you are a Holy Man, and a hermit, and also a married man?"

Krishna, at that point only, asked his wife to sit beside him. After what seemed to be an eternity to me, both of them started laughing and they laughed and laughed, rolling on the damp floor of the ancient cave as if they would laugh their heads off. Raghuvir and I sat stunned.

At that point, I stood up and signaled to Raghuvir that we should leave. Only then, Krishna came back to his senses, stood up and gave me a warm hug and said, "Life has had such unexpected and strange twists for both you and me."

VOICES FROM OLD LAHORE

"**D**r. Sonjee, please attend the annual meeting of the Pakistani Psychiatric Society in Lahore next year as my guest." Dr.Ahmed and I were attending the Annual Meeting of the American Psychiatric Association in Atlanta,Georgia. It was May of 1978. He was a prominent psychiatrist in Plakistan and representing his society at the Atlanta Convention. I had met him in one of the sessions and we connected. It was regardless of the fact that I was from India and a Hindu.At that time I had a busy private practice in Savannah,Georgia.

"Dr.Ahmed, you know I am originally from India. If I come to Lahore, I might be killed. You know very well, there has not been a closure to the 1947 partition."

"Dr.Sonjee, I assure your safety. You and I are psychiatrists. We have a commitment to treatment of the mentally ill. I understand,you have specialized in the treatment of anxiety disorders. I would like you to present a paper at our next meeting."

Dr.Ahmed was warm and genuine. Here was a Pakistani Muslim whose family had migrated from Lucknow to Lahore on the eve of partition.

"Dr.Ahmed, I will consider it. India's partition followed by wars in 1965, 1971 and the creation of Bangladesh have caused bitterness that is simmering on both sides, but with people like you in Pakistan, however, I see a glimmer of hope. I will consider your suggestion. Yes, I would love to pay a visit to Lahore. According to ancient Hindu traditions, the city was named after Lav, son of Rama of the epic Ramayana, an incarnation of Lord Vishnu."

At the end of the Atlanta convention, I invited Dr.Ahmed to Savannah on his next trip to America.

His was a friendly invitation, perhaps incidental. But, I was surprised to receive a reminder to mail a paper for the January 1979 program in Lahore. I was not sure I would undertake such a trip, but the invitation was tempting, as an educational trip on cross-cultural psychiatry plus visiting a historic city.

Time went by and I had to make a decision.I wrote to Dr.Ahmed explaining my mixed feelings, but again, I heard from him assuring me of my safety in Lahore.

I was received with so much warmth in the Lahore Airport on that beautiful, cool morning in January. Dr.Ahmed introduced me to his parents, wife, two adult children, their families and a few members of the Pakistani Psychiatric Society.

With such a warm welcome, I was no longer apprehensive. It was a joyous group, everyone talking at the same time. I was the center of attraction and I greeted everyone. We left for the Lahore suburb of Gulberg, where Dr.Ahmed and his family lived. I was to stay in the family home.

Dr.Ahmed had arranged an elaborate and tight program for me and considering that I was a history buff, I would be in guided tours for at least a couple of days.

Lahore, in some way, looked like parts of Delhi. Dr.Ahmed accompanied me everywhere introducing me to his friends. During these tours, we visited the Shalimar Gardens laid out by Shah Jahan in 1641, three terraces with more than four hundred fountains. We visited the marvellous tomb of Jahangir. Everywhere I went and met people, I was greeted with much warmth, even if people knew that I was originally from India and a Hindu.

In the family home of Dr.Ahmed,we talked about everything except partition of India. I even talked about my childhood days in a small town in Orissa, our Hindu festivals, rituals and ceremonies. Mrs. Ahmed was a highly educated lady with a Masters in History from the University of Punjab.She was a most charming hostess,very outgoing and talkative. Usually, Dr. Ahmed's father was quiet but on this particular evening, he started talking about his childhood days in Lucknow.

"Dr.Sonjee, have you been to Lucknow? If not, you should make a trip to that lovely city. I was born there in 1908. I would like to visit my birthplace one more time before I die. In fact I will not mind if I die there, where my parents and grandparents are buried."

At this point,the elder Ahmed started sobbing. There was a stunning silence. None rose to console him, probably because it was a shocking statement. The elder Ahmed continued,"Dr.Sonjee, our house was not too far from the great Imambara. My earliest memories are associated with this meeting place for Shi'a Muslims, and especially our celebration of Muharram. Dr.Sonjee,you are going to India after your Lahore visit. Why not take me with you on a visit to Lucknow?" Again, he started sobbing and began , beating his chest with his fists. At this point, Dr.Ahmed, Mrs.Ahmed, and I immediately responded and hugged him tightly. All of us started crying. We were speechless.

Dinner was announced. We settled down to an uneasy silence. Mrs. Ahmed started talking about the various cultural activities of Lahore. Actually, as I found out later, she was born in Lahore. She said, "I have never been to India, Dr.Sonjee. My husband was only fifteen when he left Lucknow. He has told me a lot of stories about that beautiful city." She started laughing at this point and added, "If you take my father-in-law on a trip to Lucknow, l would like to come along."

At this point, I stood up, raised my glass of water and offered a toast to the elder Ahmed, " Sir, your heart remains in India. Lucknow, according to Hindu tradition, was founded by Lakshman, the brother of Lord Rama of Ayodhya. Your city later on became a center for Islamic Art and Culture.You may not be able to visit Lucknow but I will, and on your behalf, will take bouquets to the graves of your parents and grand parents."

At this, both Dr.Ahmed, his wife and elder Ahmed started crying. They came over, hugged me but said nothing. I thought to myself, here was a Hindu in the Pakistani city of Lahore, in a Muslim home, being embraced almost like a son and brother.

As a part of the program,we made a trip to the mental hospital. Dr.Ahmed, Dr.Hussain, Superintendent of the Hospital and I visited every ward.we informally chatted with the nursing staff .Obviously, word had gone out that I was originally from India. However, I was met only with much friendliness and warmth.

Dr.Hussain stopped to greet a patient sitting in a corner of a room talking to himself.

"Sardarji, how are you today?"

I was a bit surprised at this, as I didn't expect any Sikh patients in a Pakistani mental hospital after thirty two years of partition from India.

Dr.Hussain told us that Sardarji had schizophrenia and had been in conitinuous residence as a patient since 1939.

Dr.Hussain again asked, "Sardarji, don't you want to be transferred to a hospital in India?"

At this point, Sardarji stood up and came near us. He said, "Dr.Hussain, I have told you many times I am in India. What is this Pakistan ? I do not know what it is.You have told me that this is a new country. I hear voices of Mother India every day and she tells me that she cannot be partitioned. Lahore is my home. If you send me to another hospital, I will just die."

Dr. Hussain informed us that Sardarji,the Sikh patient, had declined to be repatriated to India and as an exceptional case, had been allowed to stay in the hospital in Lahore.

I felt uncomfortable at this conversation,which had probably occured many many times. Dr.Hussain said that he was going to keep Sardarji under his care.

My paper at the scientific meeting of the Pakistani Psychiatric Society was well received.It was on post-traumatic stress disorders. Questions were raised as to such disorders on both sides of the border as a result of partition of India in 1947.

While visiting the various historic places in the city, and conversing with people, I had the feeling that this city had lost its soul, that people of Lahore had buried their historic culture and past , stories of Maharajah Ranjit Singh and Jahangir. Both are buried in Lahore. I decided to share my feelings one evening at the dinner table. "Mrs. Ahmed, you are a student of history. You know the multi-cultural and the rich multi-religious history of your city. I just have the feeling that voices of old Lahore have been silenced forever. What is your opinion?"

Mrs. Ahmed was quick to respond

"Dr.Sonjee, you are right. This Pakistan, the so-called Land of the Pure, is on the verge of disaster and suicide. Yes,we are in the process of eliminating our memories of that culture,which was so vibrant. In the name of Islam,we are bringing in barbarism, pure and simple. Look at my father-in-law. Though he migrated from Lucknow, his heart is there. If Pakistan is the Land of the Pure, how many Muslims from India are coming over?

In fact, it may be the other way, Pakistanis wishing to migrate to India."

"Mrs.Ahmed, the origins of Hinduism can be traced back to Mahenjodaro and Harappa in Sind,to 2500 BC. Your Punjab was the cradle of ancient Aryan culture for centuries. Now Kashmir is an inferno, a living hell."

Dr.Ahmed responded, "Dr. Sonjee, India should hand over Kashmir to Pakistan as it is a Muslim majority state."

Mrs. Ahmed realized that it was getting sensitive and decided it was prudent to change the subject.

"Dr.Sonjee, there has been an invitation for you to give a talk to the students of the Government College. It is my alma mater. Will you be willing to talk about mental impairments and treatment at a general level ? This is the subject the student body president has suggested."

"I will be delighted to do it. When is it ?"

"It is at 11 AM on January 26. I will take you there. I know a number of faculty members,who will have a reception for you at 10. Among them will be the principal of the college, who was born in Delhi. Several faculty members have relatives in India."

"Mrs.Ahmed, I hope they realize that I do not live in India. While I keep in touch with relatives, friends and events in India, I have been in America for many years."

The reception at the faculty lounge was extraordinarily warm and friendly. There were questions and comments about India and America. The principal wanted me to visit a certain section of old Delhi where he was born. He entertained me with many stories of his childhood,including activities with his Hindu friends. I really enjoyed this get-together.

I was escorted by the principal, Mrs.Ahmed and several other faculty members to the lecture hall.I was received by the president of the students' union.The lecture hall was full. I was introduced briefly by the principal as a psychiatrist from America. There was another welcoming statement from the president of the union, introducing me as a physician who had specialized in the treatment of social phobias and anxiety disorders.

I gave a talk for about twenty minutes on the broad classifications of mental disorders in general, diagnostic criteria and treatment.

For another thirty minutes or so,there were a number of questions on various aspects of mental health. I thought it went fairly well. I was ready to sit down as the principal got up to terminate the meeting, when I noticed a commotion in the back of the hall. I saw about a dozen youths entering the front of the hall, shoving and pushing others on their way.They stood right in front of the panel and their leader directed a question to me.

With a sarcastic tone, he asked, "Dr. Sonjee, you are a Hindu, aren't you ? Do you worship that ugly-pot-bellied elephant God Ganesh or something like that?"

I knew there was tension and violence in the air. The principal stood up and very politely stated, "Dr.Sonjee is a psychiatrist.Please do not raise irrelevant questions. Our time is up. I am sure he will stay behind to answer any questions on mental health."

The leader just laughed loudly and looked back at the audience and exclaimed, "Here is a Hindu, a non-believer, an infidel coming to Pakistan, the Land of the Pure."

Suddenly, the crowd burst into cheers.

The leader turned around and directed another comment to me,

"Dr.Sonjee, do you know what Jihad means ? It is holy war against the Hindus. You Hindus believe in re-incarnation. Let me tell you I am Aurangzeb, the Mughal Emperor reborn."

At this statement, the crowd became hysterical and I heard the slogan, "Dr.Sonjee ko Maro" which meant, something like, "Kill him."

The principal was paralyzed with fear and at this point, several rocks were thrown towards us and one hit my right arm. In a flash, Mrs.Ahmed shielded me totally from flying rocks. My only thought at the moment was, 'I may not get out alive from Pakistan.' Rock pelting and sloganeering such as, 'Kill the Hindu' and 'Holy war against the Hindus' went on for a few minutes. There was total chaos and pandemonium. Mrs.Ahmed kept whispering into my ears, "I will protect you regardless of what happens to me."

Then, just like that, the noise abated and rocks stopped coming. I heard some slogans, but it was getting less noisy. Apparently, the crowd was dispersing.

Out of the corner of my eyes, I saw policemen. My shirt was wet and I saw that it was bloody. I didn't know whose blood it was. The rock hitting my right arm did not cause that severe an injury. I hadn't felt blood oozing at that site. At this point, l heard a police officer saying, "Dr. Sonjee, are you all right ?" I was speechless. He was slowly pulling Mrs.Ahmed away from me. I saw that she was bleeding mostly from her back and arms. However, she was fully conscious and her first question to me was,"Are you all right ?" There were a number of police and faculty members surrounding us.The principal, I found out, was severely injured and had been taken to a hospital.

The officer told us, "Mrs. Ahmed and Dr. Sonjee, we will take you to the hospital for any necessary treatment. It turned out that Mrs.Ahmed's injuries were not serious and needed only out-patient treatment. Both of us were discharged and taken to Dr.Ahmed's house by police escort. I stayed a couple more days in Lahore until my flight to Delhi. Mrs. Ahmed bounced back rapidly to her usual self. There was no discussion of what happened in that college gathering, as Dr.Ahmed and I were subdued.

The same people came to see me off at the Lahore Airport. I had gotten all the details from the elder Ahmed about his parents' and grand-parents' graves in Lucknow. I went up to him.

" Sir, I will visit your parents' and grand-parents' graves in Lucknow. I have never been to a Muslim graveyard anywhere, but I will definitely go to this one."

He hugged me and said, with tears in his eyes, "Just as you Hindus wish to die in Varanasi, I wish to die in Lucknow, but it is not going to happen."

I hugged Dr.Ahmed and thanked him for his hospitality.

"Please come with your wife to Savannah on your next visit to the States." He was speechless with gratitude. Then I went to Mrs.Ahmed and held her hands. She hugged me, held me very tightly and started sobbing on my shoulders. I too started sobbing. When she let me go, I found almost everyone sobbing. Boarding of the flight was being announced.

In front of the group, I bent down, touched the soil of Indo-Pakistan and said, "I touch my forehead like a son touching his mother's feet and placing the blessings on his forehead."

GLOSSARY

ASHRAM: A secluded place for Hindus leading a life of simplicity and meditation.

AURANGZEB; sixth Mughal Emperor of India,known for his anti-Hindu policies and destruction of Hindu temples. Historians consider him responsible for the ultimate disintegration of the Mughal Empire.

AUSCHWITZ: Nazi concentration camp during World War II.

AYAHAS: Native nurse-maids.

BHAAGAVATA: Popular Hindu mythological tales.

BHAGAVAD GITA: Sacred Hindu text.

BLACK GOD: Oriyas affectionately call Jagannath, 'Kalia', meaning the'Black One.'

BRAHMIN: Priest class in the Hindu social order.

BULLOCK CART: Carts pulled by bullocks,still used in India to transport goods.

CALCUTTA: Capital of British India, 1757-1929.

CAR FESTIVAL AT PURI: Famous festival in the pilgrimage city of Puri in Orissa. Jagannath, the Lord of the universe along with his sister and brother, are taken out in processional cars. This festival is now held in several American cities.

DACOITS: Robbers and burglars

DHAULI COMPLEX: Buddhist antiquities in Orissa.

DISTRICT: Equivalent to a county.

DISTRICT MAGISTRATE: Chief Administrative Officer of a district in India.

DOWRY DEATHS: Homicides of young brides occuring in India as related to non-delivery of money or goods promised to the husband.

EMPEROR ASHOKA: Embraced Buddhism after a bloody victory over Kalinga (modern Orissa) in the third century BC.

FESTIVAL OF NEW RICE: similar to Thanksgiving of America.

GANGES: Sacred river in Hinduism.

GANDHI, MAHATMA: Father of India's Independence and the greatest spiritual leader of the 20th century.

GANDHI, INDIRA: Prime Minister of India, 1966-77 and 1980-84; not related to Mahatma Gandhi.

GITA: Same as Bhagavad Gita.

GOVERNOR-GENERAL: Chief Administrative Officer of British India until 1858.

HARI-KA-CHARAN GHAT: Literally meaning, a stairway to the river for ritual bathers,this one means,"with God's footprints."

HARAPPA: Site of pre-Hindu civilization, about 2500 BC, now in the province of Sind in Pakistan.

HARDWAR: Place of pilgrimage for Hindus in the foothills of the Himalayas and where the River Ganges enters the plains.

HINDOOSTAN: An old name for India, meaning the land of the Hindu.

IMAMBARA: A meeting place for Shi'a Muslims, a grand antiquity in the City of Lucknow, India.

JAGANNATH: Meaning Lord of the Universe, representing Vishnu, one of the Trinity of Hindu pantheon; Temple at Puri is one of the four most sacred places of pilgrimage.

JAHANGIR: Fourth Mughal Emperor known for promoting art.

JAI, JAI, Jagannath: Hail to the Supreme God.

JAINISM: an offshoot of Hinduism, resembling Buddhism, founded about 500 BC, teaches respect for all creatures.

JAWAHARLAL NEHRU: First Prime Minister of independent India.

JIHAD: Islamic Holy War against nonbelievers.

KALI: In Hindu mythology, one of the many titles of the wife of Shiva, Hindu God of Destruction; other names are Durga, Parvati, Uma and Bhawani.

KARMA: Hindu concept of Destiny.

KRISHNA: An incarnation of Vishnu.

KUMBHA MELA: Holy gatherings, the largest one now is held near Allahabad every twelve years. The festival goes back to pre-historic times.

LAV: Son of Rama, seventh incarnation of Hindu God Vishnu.

LUCKNOW: Capital of the modern Indian State of Uttar Pradesh. It is a center of Islamic culture, art and antiquities.

MAHARAJAH RANJIT SINGH: Last Independent King of Punjab in northwestern India, until the British conquered his Kingdom in the mid-19th century. Punjab State is now divided between Pakistan and India.

MAHENJODARO: Similar as Harappa.

MANTRA: An incantation or invocation as in Hindu ceremonies.

MARAHATTAS: (also, Marathas) Followers of Shivaji, Hindu Chieftain who fought Aurangzeb. They carved out independent Hindu Kingdoms following the collapse of the Mughal Empire.

MATHA: Religious order.

MATHURA and VRINDABAN: Places associated with Krishna mythology.

MOGHULS: Babur started the Mughal Empire in 1526 A.D.

MONASTERY OF SEVEN WAVES: One of the very early monasteries in the temple city of Puri.

MUHARRAM: Religious festival observed by the Muslims.

NAMASKAR: Greeting a person with folded hands.

ORISSA: A State in the eastern part of India.

ORIYA: People and the language of Orissa.

PARVATI: Consort of Lord Shiva, a God of the Hindu triad.

PRAYAG: Confluence of three sacred Rivers near Allahabad: Ganges, Jamuna and the mythical Saraswati; ash collected from the cremation site is dispersed at this spot in an elaborate ritual. Hindus believe that the Soul is thus freed.

PUNJAB: The British Province of Punjab was partitioned between India and Pakistan in 1947.

RAMA: See Lav above.

RAMAYANA: One of the two great epics of the Hindus with Lord Rama as the main character.

SAHIB: Respectful word while greeting a British Officer.

SAL TREES: A tree common in India valued for its durable timber.

SANNYASIN: A Hindu female monk.

SATI: A Hindu widow, planning to immolate herself on the husband's funeral pyre.

SATI DAHA: Hindu custom of immolation of a widow, banned by the British Government in 1829.

SATLAHADI MATHA: A monastery in the temple town of Puri.

SHAH JAHAN: The fifth Mughal Emperor of India, 1628-1658, better known as the builder of the Taj Mahal.

SHI'A MUSLIMS: Followers of one of the two great sects of Muslims. They consider Ali, the Prophet Mohammed's son-in-law, as the first Imam.

SHIVA: Hindu God of Destruction, one of the Trinity.

SIKH: A follower of Sikhism, which started as a sect of Hinduism, but now considered a separate religion. Sikhs believe in one God.

SIND: A province of modern Pakistan.

SITAL SASTHI: Marriage festival of God Shiva and Parvati, held anuually in the city of Sambalpur in western Orissa.

SONG OF THE LORD: Bhagavad Gita.

SUN TEMPLE OF KONARAK: A huge temple complex of exquisite architecture and sculpture in the state of Orissa, built in the thirteenth century for the Sun God by the King Languala Narasingha Dev.

SWAMI: A Hindu religious teacher.

SWARGADWARA: Literally meaning the'Gateway to Heaven', a cremation site at the beach in Puri; rich Hindus prefer to be cremated there.

VANAPRASTHA: Phase of retreat and detachment from active life.

VISHNU: The Preserver in Hindu Trinity.

YAMA: Hindu God, King of the underworld and the appointed judge and punisher of the dead.

ORDER FORM

Name_____

Address_____

City/State/Zip_____

Phone_____

Enclosed is my check or money order for US $18.45.
($14.95 for *ADVENTURES and MISADVENTURES of DR. SONJEE* and $3.50 for Shipping & Handling).

Indian Rs. 250
Canadian $23.00
United Kingdom £10

Send to: Snehalata Press
1353 Heather Lane, SE
Salem, OR 97302 -1525

In India: Available from:
Writer's Workshop
Uditnagar,Orampara
Rourkela-769 012 , Orissa

COMMENTS FROM EARLY READERS

The story "Voices from Old Lahore" is the perfect story to conclude your book as it ties together so many themes from the other stories. Dr. Sonjee's unguarded openness to strangers, and theirs to him is repeated in story after story. Here Dr. Sonjee opens himself to Dr. Ahmed, his wife, the doctor's elderly father, and so many other Pakistanis. The taking of time to listen to others—something we Americans need to hear, is also a highlight. This final story also takes a look at the bitter division between Pakistan and India—a problem replicated all over the world and throughout the ages with Ireland, Israel/Palestine, Bosnia, Chechnya, Cambodia, Korea, the Hundred Years War, etc. The list could go on and on. Here we have "enemies" loving and protecting one another as brothers and sisters. Bravo!

Linda Hathaway Bunza

I find Dr. Pati's stories intriguing and illuminating in the ways that his characters must often move in both the modern and the traditional Hindu world at once. Pati's stories give us valuable insight into the thinking of Indians who simultaneously live in America and in India.

Geronimo G. Tagatac
Short story writer

It is a fantastic story [The Woman From Georgia]. I liked it immensely. All these days it has haunted me. If it will be made into a movie, it will definitely impress the international audience.

Sarat Chandra Pujari
Filmmaker